The Black King of Kalfour

Robin Wyatt Dunn

JOHN OTT

SAN DIEGO, CALIFORNIA

2019

ISBN - 978-1-940830-26-1

LOC - 2018912036

Cover art by Barbara Sobczyńska

By Robin Wyatt Dunn

POETRY

Poems from the War
Science Fiction: a poem!
Sunsborne
Wine Country
What Black Delirious Daylight Sets You Forward in the Boat
Remarriages
Debudaderrah

NOVELS

Los Angeles, or American Pharaohs
My Name is Dee
Fighting Down into the Kingdom of Dreams
Line to Night Island
A Map of Kex's Face
Julia, Skydaughter
Conquistador of the Night Lands
White Man Book
Colonel Stierlitz
Black Dove
City, Psychonaut
2DEE
This Isn't One of the Stories I Remember

SHORT STORIES

Dark is a Color of the Day

PLAYS

Last Freedom

FILMS

A Wilderness in Your Heart
Party Games
American Messenger

for Mrs. Garrison

My name is

This is my testimony.

I am not sure how my story reaches you—is it in a book? Well, it doesn't matter. So much of me is dead; and I know parts of this narrative will be destroyed by my masters.

Alice, I still love you, whatever else they may make me say.

Imagine the last night of your life: the ocean is below you, rising in waves as the orbital generator turns much of it to steam. Inside your vessel, your employers are explaining to you why you will never be able to return home again.

I am an explorer. That is my profession by trade, though by hobby I am a poet. Poetry has also been one of the few things to keep me sane, in my encounters with the aliens of this earth.

They like to joke that aliens are just like you and me, but they're not. That's why we're out here; to find out: what it means that the planet is no longer in the same position that I knew as a boy, in orbit around the Sun.

Well, of course it is still there. That is one of the things I am obligated to say. All is well, with your and your children. Eat, and be merry, and pray.

Now let me entertain you with the story of The Black King of Kalfour and his daughter Effie.

1.

I've changed my mind; that is a bad story, and likely you have heard it already. I'll tell you how I became an explorer instead.

In the old books, the young man gazes out at the sea, desperate for the day that he too will be able to sail beyond the horizon. But it wasn't like that for me. You could say that it was something I was forced into; like sailors impressed into service. One night, you're out drinking with a new friend, and the next thing you know, you're halfway to Shanghai.

Well. Let me just tell you what I mean. I have been enslaved for thirty-five years, in another dimension which connects to ours through dreams. I am still trying to escape. But before I do that, I have to find my wife.

2.

I did meet the Black King of Kalfour. He wasn't black, and he had no daughter. He was one of the first who taught me how to return to Earth through effigies.

3.

I was looking for her in the alleyways, perched in the doll on the back of Mr. Stevenson, a very old school kind of British gentleman, dressed in grey with a carefully manicured moustache, marching through the slums of Karachi.

"Ask them," I whispered in his ear.

"Who am I looking for," he said.

"She has blonde hair. She's beautiful. Her eyes are grey."

"She may no longer be alive."

"Ask them."

He bends to whisper into the ears of the beggars. Overhead the US planes are dropping propaganda pamphlets, to prepare for the invasion.

I figure in the plans of my masters as a marble in a maze, tumbled about in their eager hands.

"Tell her you represent the United States," I whisper to him.

"I can't do that."

"Do it."

The people are watching the crazy man speaking to his doll; clearly a victim of evil ghosts.

"I represent the United States of America," he says to the girl, and she lets out a blood-curdling scream and I start to laugh. I am only a six inch straw doll but still quite audible.

"Do come inside, sir," she says, recovering herself, and we step into her home under the watchful eye of her father, who holds a huge machete.

4.

The marriage was ordinary, by the California seaside. She wore flowers in her hair. I wore a tuxedo. The officiant was a hippie priest and notorious drunk who we had befriended five years earlier.

Sometimes I have thought the various masks women wear are themselves gateways into the hive I have been tumbling around in ever since—that women know something about this place instinctively. I still don't know. But Alice knew, I know that. She knew much earlier than I how far we would have to travel.

How far away is it from your hand that holds the pebble to the pond where you will toss it? Is it a yard? Ten? A thousand yards? A dozen universes. Into the pond your pebble drops and the ripples spread out, like pleasure over her face in our bed, sinking us deeper and deeper into the man who I've become.

Some men take pleasure in many women; and I still dream of becoming that man, who can leave anyone at a moment's notice, for another, to survive.

But I am not he. As the wives of the men in Soviet Russia arrested by the Checka and sent to Siberia often followed them into exile, I followed Alice out of the world and into our dreams.

"You must explain yourself," the father is saying to Mr. Stevenson, and then I open my mouth and speak.

"I am a spirit from another dimension haunting this plane. My servant is missing and I must have her returned. Describe her Stevenson."

He is sweating heavily but manages to open his mouth.

"Blonde. A blonde American woman. With grey eyes. Pretty, and young."

"I know she has been here," I say. "Tell me."

5.

The arc pattern of my awareness stretches over the sky, beneath the heavy bellies of my enemies, shapes as dark grey clouds full with rain.

I will close my eyes and I will find my power, hiding somewhere inside my chest.

I will see the shining light, with or without my love. I know that.

But I still want her, desperately.

6.

In the drum of my belly I am running, over the sea of grass with my brothers, waiting for the adjutant to signal she has been spotted in the rocks and snow, freshly fallen in the night.

Each mountain surrounding our wolf bodies moves under my eyes, holding my head for the dive into the snow.

Shush

shush shush shush shush

The black light of dawn is itself the earth's, moved as a stone over the painting of the white horizon, my brothers' bodies as trees, roots scratching the sky.

I will find her but the question is the cost; how much of me will be left?

In my dreams I am the Black King of Kalfour, reigning over the Black Ocean the same as my five thousand forefathers, immobile and insane. When I wake, it is raining, and my brother is licking my face.

"Time to go," he says, and we climb the rocks, smelling her in the distance.

Stories mean knowledge, whose burden is pain and memory, and the things that we make once we know how.

That storytellers are therefore torturers is well known, but like our wolf god we reserve a reason: to say where it is we must go.

7.

I can see her but it is just a puff of snow.

8.

As though it were a duty I arm my slaves and enter into the cabin, ticking my thumb against one of their carapaces while I wait for the airlock to pressurize.

One two three one two three one two three

It's beautiful; the maze

You can almost convince yourself it's duty; or, failing that, some kind of necessary experiment in which you are an important actor. And this is almost the truth, as you lean into the path of the laser beams and work your metal platoon into the basement of another corporate coup bankrolled across four gravity wells and centering around some absurd bet made in Antwerp and you're on fire, literally on fire but your suit is fireproof; and then the bomb goes off.

Poof.

Who centers my gravity a stone under your long hereafter, my darling; is it you? What metal face shunted under the star glowing right underneath my faceplate knows me; knows me again?

Is it like last time?

Wolf or soldier of fortune; flesh or spirit.

Is it my flesh or is it my spirit? Is it my balls or is it my balls of fire?

Under the sun; inside my Neomachean maze; under your lips.

We were trying to nab a little alien technology,

me and the drones—they're all on fire now and I'm alone in space . . .

Lost in space, Mr. Robinson, you beautiful sweetheart, now get this right for the recording because I want to make sure the kids have an accurate picture of it for their Saturday morning cartoons:

Picture this . . .

The aliens control your mind.

A machine controls your body.

And somewhere way out beyond the sun you remember some part of why you came; and how you can get out; it slips under your pia mater, that's the fleshy membrane in between your brain and your skull, kids, and it says:

What if it's all a dream?

This is what we call a cliché, kids, where the hero wakes up and it's all a dream, except in the cliché it's okay, because the dream isn't real in the same way that waking life is . . . except here kids it's the reverse: dreams are more real than anything else.

So you have to ask yourself:

Just what is it that I want to do?

For me, it's find my wife. No matter what may have happened to her. Dead or alive. Enslaved or imprisoned. With another man, or in another body. The low heartache plaza of field guns and grey ornaments on the space stations of my dreams is no threat to my body, still spasmically seeking you, because it's all I have left:

I leave the transponder on one of my little metal slaves' torso, still shiny from the factory, and slip back into the mother realm where my masters are awaiting my report:

9.

Master master overload it's well it's done my heart and my reward dear master this is my spite and spear my Albert Speer this is my epitaph my winter work and won; give me my daily bread, master, or at least give me some idea of how I can get out of here . . .

"You're talented, soldier. We like watching you work."

"It's not time yet is it?"

"No, not yet."

"How long have I been here, boss?"

"Not long. There's a lot to do."

I can see something in his eye . . . some part of that thing I remembered . . . that part of the story that is most necessary . . .

What is the most necessary part of a story?

The beginning or the end? The people in it? The places? The feeling of it? What shape does the knowledge take in its container and what is its most essential element?

Flesh spirit and somnambulant war; give me fire, master, and I will light you aflame:

10.

As we begin to break away, you can feel the iceberg lift; unleashed from its moorings under the sea.

Talia is laughing and I with her; there is no substitute for the luxury of late civilization.

I hug the freezing rock with my cheek; waiting for home.

Home is so near by, as near as her lips; though she may be dead, for all I know.

Each aspect of the world needs my attention; in my investigation there is nothing that is not a clue because it all leads inward to the mining vessel of my masters, whose modus operandi is perception itself.

Of course the summa qua non of perception is predation; these apparati who predominate our head lead us to put food in our mouths and keep alive, keep the guts stirring, keep the eyes blinking, keep the mind wondering, the soul lurking beneath surface of my dear holiday; dear, won't you come with me on my dear holiday, so far away now, I promise you it's close, no nearer far, no yesterday, but here, with me.

This is the silence of my awareness in the deep silence of ocean's death, my mirror of the void in a woman's laugh, and the sound of the sea, not even angry with me yet for it knows everything.

I dive into it and huddle under the embrace

of the earth; so near now I can taste it, and what urgency should she feel, O Wanderer Happy and Bright, Dear falling Fomenting and Eager, Here Tower of Spirals and Non-Entities, Her Oligarchic May Rounds, bright as a demon, glittering and gold and ominous, my earth now dead but still afeared of living, shadow and ghost under my sighs:

"Are you still awake?"

"Yes."

Awake; even now I cannot tell which it is. Am I awake or asleep?

"I'm awake," I say.

But I'm falling.

Falling asleep awake; falling awake who is the comeuppance of my lust; the figure of my child.

Well:

The stars are close by; I could map them with the technology they've provided me but it's irrelevant; I'll only be somewhere else before I can tell.

Predation is eating, of course; is transmogrification; Ovid and his metamorphoses is life and change; we know this; I know this; but it isn't enough; it doesn't answer my question, which is:

Where is my wife?

11.

In the dark I can feel her breathing, strumming in a nightmare soufflé, coming up; she's coming up, to surface, in the dark water, the Earth:

Who
Who is it
Who
Who is it
Who cometh under me my love
My love
My love
(She says on the bus)
50p, my love
Now hop on board, my love
My love, my love
Away
We are away
I am away, Earth. Am I away?
Oh
Oh, what is it

(As the tick understands its host, I understand the Earth)

She came to me in the night when I was a girl, still hot with love, burning in the bright sky, she passed over me and told me the way, in the night, when I was still a girl, burning with love.

He who passes the night over me gives me a wishes, gives me a wishes, gives me to wishes, for an hour, to spite through and see the shape of me,

who I am, for me, now persevering, now hereafter-
ing my self, so dear and new, now old and bark and
bread; so new and in intent the sky should shake
me under its demon grasp, like a lover of the old
board, now recumbent, succulent and to the test,
my ocean tastes the cum and soup, the goop and
chirp and chirrup harp, you ominous hue, grew off
of me; grew onto me; grew new.

He who barks the old island should subsume
who would consume the broom dream skyward
and sell me the fit; I will have it; sell me the fit,
five thousand dollars, ten thousand lifetimes; I will
have it; I will have your fit and raise you one; I
will have it fitting; I will have it fitting right, the
glipe and glider, tent and strider, on my gut, who
art my name, who art wintering my name so bold
and organic great tastic splinter and frantic glider
my glider, be real to me, if you are me; be real to
me; if you knew me; my love;

12.

Once I knew the Black King of Kalfour in his Black Kingdom; in his Black Kingdom where all go to die; where I too am dead, and grieving; where I will not be revived. I am both things; dead in the kingdom of the king, and here with you, writing, reading, telling this story of how I found my wife in the stars.

Now when I knew the Black King of Kalfour in his Black Kingdom I was still a boy, and not yet a man, and all the things that men know were not yet privy to me, so I believed that the Black King of Kalfour in his Black Kingdom would be something near to forever, as a child passes a year in the emptiness of grief, for all years are grief to a child.

In the year of grief with the Black King, there in Kalfour, it's true I became a man, but I did it later; later than I should have; later than I wanted to. I wanted to do so much.

In the Kingdom of Kalfour the Black King grows weary and he tells stories, stories to last an age, perhaps two; perhaps forever, if he likes; he can do that. He can do anything; I know it; it is as though I am his child, though I am not. I have no father; and will never have. Nor am I an orphan. My mother is the Earth, now dead.

In the Black Kingdom of Kalfour I knew a secret: I was alive, though dead. And I am still, writing this to you. I who will never die. I who am with you; dying; I am with you; dreaming; give me to you; as I give you to me; nourishment in the storm of our lives.

13.

Well, I've been away a long time. I'm sorry. Coming back isn't easy; you know that. All the changes that have come, the biggest one being in me.

We're working on the canal through the city; digging, and digging, and digging. Los Angeles, with already one Venice, plans to become many.

That the Pacific will not pacify the population is obvious; but they do try.

One is tempted to arrive at meanings, to assume and then assign the meaning to what has occurred, and describe the events in the light of this assumption, so as to create a story that will be easy.

Easy stories, like easy women, aren't ever really what interested me.

Still, the meaning comes anyway, not from me. It is some other thing, over me, near by to me, and, very slightly, within. The change in me is not the meaning; that is accidental, or just a side effect. The meaning is larger than that; some demon ghost who has arrived from another dimension and now insists on his right to play. Come, I will play with you, he says. This is how it will go.

Jump up, jump down, jump up jump up and get down, and run away from yourself, into my mighty evening, from which there can be no escape, until I let you go.

This is how stories function for me, like possessions of spirits. They can be exorcised but it is better not to; because their only real exorcism is in the telling.

I don't understand how Los Angeles is still alive; Hollywood is long gone, along with any semblance of an economy, yet so many did not leave. I suppose it's, as they say, the weather. Even when it's near impossible to find anything to eat sometimes.

We're digging, and watching the water seep through our shoes.

"Hey did you hear what they said?"

"What?" I say.

"They said we're gonna be done at noon. No more canal."

"I thought we were going all the way downtown."

"Some cockup in the Big House; Dame Big Nose is upset."

"What a shame; I was starting to enjoy this."

"Hahahaha!"

But we keep digging. Why stop. The shovels are still here, and the dirt. The water and the sun. And somewhere nearby is my wife. I can almost smell her. With my mind. Even with my nose.

So luminous the regard of the sun; Lucifer or Ahura Mahzda, Sol and Solaris rolled into one, my body as an estuary caught in the kelp of Earth, unable to escape, nor wanting to, and pulled into the edge of its body . . .

"We're done!" my coworker says, and I follow him back to the shelter, the lean-to in the grass where we've been smoking.

Somewhere in the distance I can hear the bell ringing; they'll bring water.

The sun is a kind of metronome, humming over the orchestra-in-training of the Earth, subsiding and rising, rising and subsiding to suggest but not impose an order; sending its signal over the dark.

Here, here now, come back; I am with you. This is me, here with you; light.

I've been away; far away. So far I can't even describe it, though I would like to. Tell me, what have you seen? Has it been interesting? One of my cousins made you, in his belly, and it makes me curious, who you are. It's not that I have some ownership over you; far from it. It's just that I need you; have been needing you, ever since I first saw you.

Whose light am I, embarked and now delivered, umbrage and shade, order and amends, the fruit of the word of the dark bent under and baked and married soft full and weary, now entered into the book, lofted at right and centered on the belt for your hand; here I am. Touch me.

"Are you all right?" he asks.

"A little sunstroke maybe. Is that water here yet?"

"It's coming."

He stands and shouts: "Hey, hurry up!"

I hear them hurry; the ladle clanking against the bucket.

14.

When I was a boy the king knew me; now I am a man. Who that is is uncertain; but I do know I have been sent here, for reasons unknown to me. Still, this knowledge gets in the way of my will: that I am looking for her. That so many men (perhaps all?) should have to tolerate someone using them for other purposes even as they pursue their own aims I continue to find astonishing—astonishing that we bear it. I suppose that is part of our design. Anything else would be too selfish.

He taught me arithmetic: how to count. How to add and subtract. I'm not sure we ever got to multiplication and division. Nor have I really needed them in what I've been assigned to do:

Wait. One year and two. And three and four and five and six and seven.

Marking the angles of the sun whose radiance defines my acts, and makes them sensible. Sensible though acts in the sun, made known through the sun, arced through the sun, made visible, and made sturdy, and then brittle:

I brittle in the sun am born to you; no matter. No matter at all. We are growing here and I can assign any meaning I wish; but I do not want to draw any signs. We are a town not on the map.

Not on any map.

"He's awake."

They pour the water over my lips.

She's standing over me.

"Alice."

15.

Alice, at root, means "at the rank beyond nourishment." A noblewoman.

Is the noblewoman beyond such physical needs? Or she merely controls it for the rest? Perhaps both.

Or it could simply mean "nourishing those above."

Alice falls below to nourish those above, and in her fall we espy the logic of the transition between them, not merely gravity but a trade. Down for up. Dirt for air.

I give my dirt for her air, and she lifts me up out of the mud, somewhere in the region formerly known as California, in the body of a man who used to be David. Now I don't know who I am.

"Are you all right?"

"I am now."

She looks at me like she doesn't know who I am. And I realize then: here, she doesn't.

16.

We're moving together on the subway, towards the hospital downtown. I sit to her left, by the window, and we both stare straight ahead like strangers, which after all is what we are.

The train is crowded and someone is playing music: 'I heard it through the grapevine' performed by Jimi Hendrix.

Who heard the news, and what was it, sent through the crowd into our ear, epiphanic and boring, the mark of delivery:

"You really should wear a hat," she says.

"Yes."

The train is a sedative, decoupling the body from the mind, an invitation to destroy the fruits of your labor and subsist instead on communion: the hour unhooked from others and so singular, locked away in our tight box, undergoing sublimation.

We arrive at the hospital and I ask her to stay with me—I tell her I'm afraid, which isn't true, or maybe it is, I don't know.

To my surprise, she agrees, and we wait for my name to be called, still strangers, but now sharing a common purpose.

"How are you feeling?" the nurse asks.

"Fine."

"Any headaches?"

"No."

"Nausea?"

"No."

"Have you been drinking water?"

"Some."

"Drink more. I'll be back to take your blood in a few minutes."

Now that Los Angeles is dead—or dying—I find I like it more than I ever did, although it's possible I've fallen out of love with it.

It seems to have given this city a tiny dose of humility, the knowledge that it, too, will end.

Who shines brightly in my ear, who delivers the peace on the sunlight, to remove from me the burden of consciousness and bestow instead this feeling of calm, and spacelessness? It's California, but California is no more, so perhaps it is the ghost of California, who was here before the Spanish, and the Chumash, and will be here too long after humanity is gone.

The light itself.

The light insists that we are known—that all mutations are known—and we are this great mutation, hideously superior in our meaty claws and chitinous thumbs, enduring the light so we can slip back into darkness . . .

The nurse comes back in, and takes my blood.

- -

When I come out she's gone.

- -

The body remembers what other parts will not, of how long it's been. Who made the will wait, and the favor quiver, and the long drop to the spell, so near to me now I can kiss it with my lips—

It's a long trip back to Venice—the old Venice, well the older Venice, off the Expo Train, and down the sand past the drug addicts and B-movie stars.

We are vasted in the conviction that our force is just and that its use is slow, barely even reasonable, or careful, but so slow, you can feel it, slip over the edge, water to drain, sun to singularity, a dreadful and healing weight, of humanity.

Now I have seen her, but here she is not my wife. Perhaps that is the goal of my masters—a new kind of torture—to bring me versions of her but never my version, not the version who loves me.

We're pulled down and back, under the city, out of its way, the true city beneath the pretend city, beholden only to each other, whatever we are.

But this philanthropic sentiment is unbecoming in my dead America—better that I honor only my king, who rules in the distance, and so close, whose old eyes are the color of the sea.

- -

"Are you awake?" she says.

"Hmm."

"I'm going."

"Right now?"

She kisses me on the cheek and takes her key and locks the door behind her.

I can almost forget who I am—but no. It is a prison from whom I cannot escape.

- -

Each Los Angeles is precious to me but the dead one is perhaps best, as that one lives under the surface of all of them, as the skeleton does the body, waiting for its truth to be revealed.

I am on cleaning duty again—an impossible task in the waste. Meaningless to stack bricks in this holocaust because no one is coming to build with them.

Still, it is what I do, like a monk making sand drawings, in full knowledge of the end of the known universe.

The spirit is still waiting here, of course—like I said, it lives somehow separately from the city— perhaps the city visits it, and not the reverse.

The spirit who is patience, and madness, as all patience must be madness, and more—there can be no surfeit of it.

It is waiting for some land indescribable— likely not physical at all. It's waiting for the right word.

"What word is it, you spirit?"

17.

and now we'll fuck you; fuck you for the right one, fuck you fat and solemn shaking in the boot fuck you for a hoot a scoot across the floor the root of the truth whose moocher gave us all we ever needed; we will, I promise, fuck you for the friendship and the pattern of our demise fuck you for the loose and morose sentiment of the caboose; leaving; leaving; gone:

We'll fuck you for fun; for a laugh; for a smoke; a candle; rigid and spectacular; no hereafter; no moreover; no stand nor fate to turn you towards us nor distort our presence shaking fuming and erect; detect the song and we will sing you over the edge; stay now and wait; the break is all and we will have it, true:

we'll fuck you for an hour; when the river's done and the city doesn't know it; when the randy mixes with the fear and no tear nor tantrum will dissuade us; when the stagnant tower of desire looms a precipice before you; when the howl and hate and love the course of true affection bent to work the might and mirror of the slave the fear and field the ardor of the hour burning, churning, maiming the milk of the nose, rotundan snows around your face, no ace can count them, no mace will shake nor shirk the melon of your curse, no ruse may undertake to blame our power.

fuck you for an hour; for a day; in any way we

choose; for just a way to say that we were sorry; or were sorry and no longer are; or were sorry and now don't care at all; it's moot; a hoot; a thousand dancers without eyes

I prize your spirit and I challenge thee to make it worthwhile; on style; on mass and en masse; on the chance of the get out, heat out and stir:

Who will answer for it if we fuck you; truck you and duck you; muck you, suck you and un-stuck you from the gravel and the tenor road, it's a road piss; bliss and murk; worth the jerk and the brake to count the swords and sterile aisles, the wreck and the pearl, are one, in you:

Unlovely and true, not a game, not fun, no gun can make us shake, my love may make you do; the laugh or the choke; to mark:

Imbue me with the truth; whose ruse moves the fluid and marks the ruth to shake the bones and agitate the nonce to nose; whose more will bright the stance stay the chance to keep you; will I be enough?

- -

I don't know what the meaning is any more. Who made the world under her heart, so mer-ry or true, subdued to the light, to mean these things, now arrogant or stubborn, and now im-placable, the ruth at the heart of the earth, subter-minal, exquisite and unstoppable, like lockjaw, or articles of confederation, written not in blood but light, transmitted in all directions:

But who receives the transmission? That's me. I am your receiver. Winter now reveals the heart of the radio god, stubborn too, implacable too, harboring races and telephones and huge libraries vibrating under a helicopter solitude to demand the meaning, where is it, where has it gone, what shape moved under sigh to determine its origin, and stop the movement of breath? Which dimension of time subsists to create the corridor of our awareness, now black, grey and pearl, world white and sheened with regret?

It is each time I stand in the mirror; and each time I pass through the door away from The Black King, who is only an aspect of myself. I know that now. If I am an orphan it is of my own making. And I have only been talking to myself.

But the solipsistic monologue is not without meaning, even if it be divined only afterwards; only in translation; only in duress.

In duress the meaning fuses to the body, the words are the body, the light is the body, and I am the kingdom itself, wrought out of time and made nowhere, heaven:

18.

She rises now, covered in pearls of water, re-
splendent, and though I am dead I can feel the
weight of her, even after she has left I feel her
standing, emperor of the ages.

I am no one and so can take no offense at anything; and nowhere is bliss.

Nowhere is bliss and I am no one, dancing under a light that does not quite exist:

Rum de rum

achoo

I can feel the weight of her like no other, after I am dead, and after all harbors are closed to
me I feel this great opening; some world that was
closed to me on the earth has opened to me, a
river at its making.

River is being made, under the rock, out of the
mountain and the year, carved and ordinated for
the religion of time, making its voice strange and
quiet out of the faces of the gods, shining with
light, and trembling like naiads before the empire of it, laid solemn and quiet, empress, and her
legions, awake from the dead, soldiers of water,
made new to the night:

I am the river of the night. Weapon and scroll;
five thousand years and some bitter love affair; it
is memory itself who is watching me, freezing my
skin; giving me the trigger for the war out of my
heart.

"Are you all right?"

"Yes, I think so."

"You were talking to yourself."

"Probably I was. A bad habit."

She sits by me and looks out over the broken stonework.

"I think we should get lunch," she says.

"I'm dead; I don't eat."

"Well you can watch me eat then. There's some good peaches ripening now."

We're waiting for the sun; it is invisible.

This aspect too is merely iteration; finding her again not in memory but some thing's imagination: who the Black King knows. Who he knows is me, and Alice, exquisite Alice, who took me away from all the things I knew and, after all, taught me what I had forgotten.

"I have to tell you something," she says, swallowing the juice of the peach. "I know who you'll meet next."

"Who is it?"

"It's the Black King next."

19.

The Black King of Kalfour has an appointment at 4:30 at The Book; he cannot be late. The subway is faster for him; who wields the mighty sword; shaking it ribald over the faces of children on the train, who laugh hysterically, knowing him for the best joker of the morning.

The best joker of the morning is on the way to his desk, not to write or read or declaim but to pound on it with a hammer, made out of nails, curved and melted into a cruel and twisted bludgeon. With each blow, the office shakes, and his coworkers settle into the rhythm of it, setting their watches by his cruel blows.

The Book is a quintillion gigawatt laser originating in an office building on Wilshire, fired two arcseconds north of Canopus so as to tame the hair within the Black King's face; he is afraid of himself.

The Black King is dancing outside the front doors, holding it open for residents returning with their groceries in between his dance steps, which describe the movements between slots in the computer network of his dreams.

Whose dance ignites the city but the Black King, for to be the heart is to be singular, patient and true, and a trigger for the aegis of the sky, subnuclear and viscous, twisting the shape of the stars into dresses for the city to wear, between coffee and quitting time.

Come to the ball; it is at the Wiltern Theater in Los Angeles, under a blood red zombie sky, where the patience is a magnetic field equal to the strength of certain secret military weapons, fused around an alien ship's belt who forms the gate and metal detector before the bar and disco ball;

Equate
My mate with the truth
And your eye with the sky
We are seeking you
Behind our eyes
Where we've come to die again; the right way.

This is the right death; an aching wind. We are dancing together; Manchuria; Macabre; Machiavelli and Moltar (whose cousin was Crystar) inside a gypsy camp inside a sealed district inside an alien dictatorship controlled by a king who cannot control himself, we are dancing to the beat of the disco light show, the Montagues.

The Montagues are dancing, only ravens, only the Attic of the Attic race, fluttering furiously to get a message out and across the canyon and perhaps to the swamp, or at least Santa Monica:

The Black King is come to Kalfour to The Book and his Hammer sounds nails for the children, hammering, hammering on their tin drums for the sound of the bright sky:

The Montagues are the Tower People, the

Etruscans, bent into the hideous shape of their own protection, the Mech, and so long live the Mech, long live the Mech of the Black King and his Kalfour, where I am living now; where I am dead and dancing, the best medieval skeleton, eager and happy, and unstoppable.

Now serve me, who am old; my old and last life; I am looking for her.

Have you seen her?

She looks like this.

My name is

20.

We're shaking faster; my regalia are clattering against one another: samurai armor.

Finally I leave and go to sleep on my desk, watching the stars spin around the earth.

The leaves of the ship are uncurling and we are sailing to Madagascar; the Lemur King has called for aid and we are to give it, however we can; however incapable we may be; one must honor one's alliances even in death.

Episode means "additional entrance." And so I a corpse have been revived many times, sometimes by myself, applying the gasoline and electricity, and sometimes by others, to aid me in my ridiculous search.

Alice will fall further yet; should I escape it can hardly be as a man, but some think I gave up my manhood long ago and so I don't care about that. What is humanity but more dirt?

We are entering the Red Sea.

I am leaving; with my ship of leaves. We are the leaves of the earth, curling up under the sun, to go to Madagascar, where there are no more dreams, and no more waking, only the Lemur Labyrinth, in which I will finally get some idea of where my wife has gone.

21.

We've been going about it all wrong. Some picture of my mind is floating over the sky; weaving into it her face, even though she is here beside me.

"I'm going to look for you," I whisper to her.

"Okay," she says.

"I don't know where you are."

"I'm right here."

You could say it's our child, the cloud figure hovering over our boat, except that it's an adult face; merged her and me through the medium of this search and bonded to my eyes, flickering soft and glimmering above us over the ocean:

The Black King of Kalfour is watching us, playing checkers, slamming them down onto the board, licking his lips, pouring the whiskey into his glass, picking up the telephone and calling:

Ring ring ring

"Yes, who is it?"

I can only hear him breathing.

"What is it?"

click

Watching and listening under the tide; the sailors bear their mark and watch the horizon for sign of rain, pirates, mermaids, meteors, fighter jets and other astronomical events, bent and caped, our voyage;

Our voyage;

Our voyage;

Our voyage;

Now here; burning bright, in the forests of the night, and no hand nor eye can meet our fearful symmetry, in the dark:

What fearful symmetry is a woman, like a black pinion, struck through the brain, hoving in a field, rapturous electric, solemn wastrel scuffed and battered to the tug of the Gulf Stream, to the pull of the ocean, unmiraculous home:

My unmiraculous home take me, who art alone, undoable, redoable, bimetric, herded and well founded, unintelligible, ironic, burr and mar and sore, my evensong ripe reared and strumming though not on key or in tune, still vibrating beneath you:

Be here my love, over in the sky, be here though there is nowhere else; not until we have escaped; be here to bear my visage and I will tear the bright cards terror chords lumined rocks strong shadows and weight; well; well; won't I

"I'm still listening," the Black King observes, puffing on his pipe.

"Get off the phone," I tell him, and hang up.

"I'm still here," he says.

I close my eyes and try to sleep, listening to the place over the sky where she is.

22.

Now wild wheat inform me bent rage bent buildings holocaust inform me my minions inform me Black King my rage informs me I am the interloper and I am the prize but that is nothing; tell me; give me the secret I need to enter; give me all the secrets I need to enter.

Tell me the name of the gown and the name of the town, the temple of her fear and the strong of her hate; hate me, give me your hate; I will wear it; I need it too.

Tell me the secrets so I can go in; so I can bring my merry wastrels in; tell them it's safe; tell them we know, which door, which keep, which century and which oak, tell them I remember and will get going; tell them I understand at least a little of why we've come, where the ordinals who can raise them up, to peer our ship, through the dark.

Now wild wheat upstanding wheat Anatolian wheat black mask wheat hold hay wheat argent wheat unplanned wheat maple wheat murder wheat scraped scuffed and bonded to the truth; give me the name on your tongue, let me taste it; if you will; I shall have one of the kernels to the keep:

Name my wheat for the word; name it for my word; bury me with your word; now terrible the word; hold me; take my hand:

"You've come a long way, sailor," the siren says.

"Give me passage and I will let you enjoy my friends," I say.

"But who is it with you?"

"I am bringing a message of stone."

She smiles. "Whose stone is it?" Flashing bright colored scales over her face.

"Yours," I say, and smash her in the jaw. My men grab their swords and I plug the wire under my tongue;

humming;

humming

drum:

drum drum

drum drum drum

drum drum drum drum drum

each holocaust insists it knows the reason, for its intervention, but only I know the reason, and will have it, my holocaust Los Angeles, my buried Los Angeles, now wild, even in death, you are wild, give me, each hour, the name of your frisbee, still unthrown, still unnameable, now slipping over the edge of the grass;

Give me the task for the spirit of Los Angeles voice in the murk, please voice in the murk with me Los Angeles your voice in the murk shall voice in the murk it shall be voiced in, no better, no weather no burn, ensconced tragic and fired for the sirens:

Burning over the sky

The sirens are burning in the water outside the labyrinth Madagascar

The sirens are burning in the air over the city Los Angeles

Give me the name and I'll give you the poem

Give me the poem and I'll give you the door, to the woman:

So near . . .

"I'm listening," the Black King says.

"I know."

Give me the poem and I'll give you the reason, O Intervention Scholastical; O Invention Dead. Give me Your Death and I Will Imprison It; I Will Own it; Miraculous:

Each passage of the word bears in the word for our oars; keeps back the dark for our spark; speaks the spark for the making of the bird; we are a bird; bent down and into the dark water underneath the continent Madagascar; each passage will be; if I can; made new:

The doors move with my words; and the sailors are screaming; laughing; crying;

Make them move with my words;

Move down;

And stroke:

Make the wild wheat the key; arbor the key; Menelaus the key; bent to the work of the sword; and the work of the poem; making new:

Anatolia is coming over Los Angeles; like a

thousand tumbleweeds, moving into the Western set, mobbing the expensive cameras and the expensive actors, scrubbing them clean, to their bones;

Anatolia rises over Los Angeles; the wheat carrying the bodies, undulating the bodies, of all Men; marrying the corpses to their sisters and weeping; arbor den; shriking the pavements of Los Angeles, merging with the body of Los Angeles, terrifying the spirit of Los Angeles, my key, under the water, down to Kubla Khan and his children, down under the word beneath the world of words;

Los Angeles is Anatolia now; my hybrid.

She is rising. Rising Anatolia, over the wheat, with her golden scythe:

The water locks are rising and we guide the boat in, deeper down.

I can hear the Black King clapping.

Clap clap clap

"I applaud you king!"

"Who is he talking to?" the sailors ask.

"His gods."

Rising Anatolia over the networked Los Angeles restaurant categorical, networked categorical, humane categorical, a human wine. Human flesh on the plate. Rising Anatolia over the networked Hollywood categorical, Buddhist categorical, a quantum key under the acid tongue, paper stamp and strumming chord to dumb the winter spirit in each dead theater in Los Angeles, on parade;

All the dead Hollywood men are on parade, celebrating their death, eating their skin, setting fire to their hair, humming and dancing, with their huge grins.

I reach out and pluck a femur from his leg, and take it into my hand a sword, Boney, and the man is laughing and jumping around on his singular leg, pointing at me;

Anatolia rises over Los Angeles like a fast-motion disease, the millennia merely a wind, Ozymandias or Babylon, both, limping and spinning, spinning in Sufi white, the colors of the wheat rise over Los Angeles and I am screaming with the bone in my hand.

How many keys? Seven? Eight? Nine? Surely not ten. Or perhaps this one goes to eleven . . .

"We can hear you down there!"

"Who is it?" I shout into the dark. The sailors listen, eyes wide.

"It's Spinal Tap here, what do you want?"

"I am the shaman come to open the gates into the Lemur King's home."

"Well go away, I'm trying to sleep!"

"Please, let us in."

"Go away, I said! I have a hangover."

"My sailors can brew you up a wicked hangover cure!"

"What's in it?"

"Umm, grog."

"Hmm. Is that it?"

"And rum."

"Hmm."

"Do you require a password?"

"Yes, what's the password?" the voice asks.

I check the wire is still connected underneath my tongue.

"It's . . .

A dining room in Los Angeles! Winter bright! In the forest of the night! Where neither hand nor eye can see the Eye of Sauron and his mighty winter keeping all the plates clean and all the silver shining and all the guards dead alive.

All the wine the finest child's blood.

And all the trees dead on their stalks.

Where we can discuss the movies. The beautiful movies over their dead screens. Showing the holocaust. Every night.

In the dining room of Los Angeles we are the key makers, shining with max, speckled with bronze, grinding our keys down over the spinning stone, sparks gleaming over our cheeks and hair. Each key is a jewel we set into her hair, our princess, ensconced in the Walmart hardware department, stone and lapis lazuli, with amber eyes, burnished and gleaming under the flickering fluorescents we key makers spark the steady murmur of our fright, we spark the steady murmur of our frightened keep, making the weight, bearing the Walmart weight, each brother and sister of the Walmart Klan ever weightier, stamping their feet into the marsh, to work the gods around the keys, around her eyes, we are the key makers, deadly bright, luminous and unreal, but solid, and dedicated, to one key after key clinking and clanking a chain of the divine.

"Go away, I'm asleep!" Spinal Tap shouts.

"Pour some of that grog into the hole in the door," I tell the First Mate, and he does, and we hear the gurgling sound of the rock and roll star imbibe his hangover cure.

"Bear left!"

And we pull on the oars, and sink down:

23.

The Black King is waiting, asleep.

"Are you there yet?" he asks me.

"No."

Bend right and wait, your shoulder for the sun, who will not know how desperately you answer for it, how terrible you answer for it, stumbled and straggled shot off and comforted by the stream:

Bend right and wait, by the sun, for our poem, and we will hear it, we will move it, no matter how long it takes. It could take a very long time; but likely it will only take a few minutes.

Under the record player where the sun comes on, alight, lighting up the day—no wait, a fuse has blown, John do you have any extras? Thank you, John—*crack snazzle pop*—here comes the sun.

Bend right and weight, for your shoulder the sun moves by weight through the earth, cooking it slow to ash:

You weren't meant to bear so hard on the pedal, John.

Sorry, let me back up:

By weight towards the earth, bucking and twitching, perseverating, mad bronco sun, a diva, waiting for the right moment, and then: she opens her mouth: and light:

(light comes) out

Lights out over the night, senor, we've been

to bed and are still sailing; a good sailor can sail while he is asleep.

There is no fear, senor, for we are forever. Forever with you.

I press the receiver to my ear

He's still there, breathing regularly.

"I love you, King," I say, and hang up, and the cabin boy hands me my cigar and light it and hold it but do not smoke it; I just want to smell the tobacco.

"Do you want to smoke it, boy?"

"Aye sir," and he does. He can't be more than ten.

24.

This is a story about escape from empire, an escape many will say is not possible.

Who holds the mace over my hair;

Who is there?

The rhyme of the deep? Her merry creep unpaired: the rare and ow and hair; my air; my gorgon; my here:

Who is it scrapes the seed from off the steed of the air, the beating spate of the time and place; each man and woman endowed to the emblem of our torture, each in turn, one thousand, two one thousand, three one thousand, four, turn me around, give me a biscuit, and marry:

These times will not escape; nor will I. The best I can do is set a signal into them; to record and divest of the significance of it, and make my name, however inadequate, stoned around the circle of held hands and truths summoned over the grass:

Which is it? A woman? Which is a woman. Who art a woman. The art makes the earth; undoable; implacable; my own art, sent to nature, black and pleading; no longer a real man; or a real nomenclature; only a sound;

Muttering muttering

Who is not something that can escape from it: if you are a who, you have already agreed to be imprisoned. The question is what will be the reason for your escape, and what name you will leave behind on the door of your exit:

A stir, which concurs with the mixture it stirs, round not only the mixture itself, but the people who made it, when they fell in love with the feeling of it, men and women, now and then: indentured to the feel of the earth, each arc and each mind, each mast, kept to the willing of it, ardorous and impure, phallus for the awning of the sky:

25.

The Black King rises, like a storm, made curious and alone, singing to me:

"Have you seen her?" he asks.

"No. Yes. I've seen her."

"What are you going to do about it?"

Leap;

ten thousand floors

twenty galaxies;

the make of the marble air

each dream keep

each insignificant instant, bent to the curve of my life

quivering, colored, liquid and sticky, a shirt for the winter of this journey:

"So you've seen her?"

"Yes."

"Are you going to take her from me?"

26.

The Black King rises: a blade:

The plotting of death.

We consider murder as we consider our reflection in the mirror:

Is it just? Is it handsome? Do I remember myself? And how have I changed?

So with murder, we consider the weapons and the timing; we consider the enemy and his motives, her motives, wrapped around our ball of twine, so springy, and light:

Will it be enduring? Will it be something I have earned, as I plunge this blade into his throat?

Yes;

yes;

yes;

this is my only time, as a man.

Which art my hand; my arm and art; who art my arm and hand my art; who art with me; tell me the name of the truth and I will kill with it, for I can have no other,

The men leap out of the walls.

The cabin boy is like my son. Like the son I

never had with my wife.

To arms my son for so fell a fate will keep me warm, next to you.

Each man and each woman marries a storm, and I saw yours, like Neptune his Trident, marked and bent to his shape, never bearing, never wavering, thought itself:

Each man and each woman marries it, to the storm of the word of his name and his eyes:

Tell me;

Tell me;

Give me the reason for it; as I would give you it; and bury them in the sea.

Give me the reason for my love, and I will burn it alive, if only to spare you. I would still do that.

I would still do it for you.

Each man and each woman marries it the storm to marry themselves, if only for a week, a month, a spate of the spurt of the ocean, married to the deep, to betake themselves in the mention of it, not even after, not even coming to the story after, not even having made it that far, but for the story of it in the instant, who art also made new and old made rough and edged and bright, made my own, son, for the truth of the killing of it, for if it is my wife down here then I will have her and if you are my tool in the army of it then you are my arm and I will swing thee, sing thee, marry thee too; mar you for the world.

27.

Some of my men are dead. But the cabin boy has survived. We kick the pirates into the water as we sink further, under the water, under the tomb of the Lemur King.

We are riding him, riding the history of the Lemur King, whose story is 60 million years of kelp, as the story of Man is the story of five million years of wood.

So are we delivered over the ocean, to sink beneath it and give birth to our stories.

"Are we done, sir?" he asks.

"You were beautiful, son. A real killer."

He smiles like a man.

"Here, have a sandwich."

The water is the color of emeralds.

28.

Now things have subsided; we are in calm water. The boy is asleep; I have given him my blanket.

The darkness is soothing; I can just barely see my men. We sink slowly as in a great water lock. The only sound is the lapping of the water against the rock, and the creaking of the ship.

In darkness I can find the soothing balm I have been needing; it binds me to everything that I move towards the closer I come to forgetting. Darkness is a kind of memory which is interposed between living memory and death. Just as dream is a kind of memory. Its kingdom admits no other adherents: even if you wanted to maintain an allegiance to light, you are unable to. Darkness is totalizing in this way.

Her mystery is my salvation, a rope with which I may hang myself if I wish, or use as a belt in the robe of the order she raises about her, waters of the seventh ocean, crashing into unseen boundaries below, wetting my face.

"We're getting closer," I tell the boy. He turns in his sleep.

29.

We're all lies; I can't make it any better. If I could, I would tear you out of my head and eat you, Zeus with an aborted Athena, to eat wisdom and have it gone, no more and out of my mind, for good.

So what is it to look for a woman? Is she near-by?

And if near, who is she?

What is her mind and what story her thoughts, a body unwrought no nearer the font of birth nor death, each principle of the order of her delayed, so as to arrive syncopated onto a man's awareness, not near to breathing, nor apparent to the stride of the ape and his man, bent to the will of it, near-er now but no clearer, apparent to god but he is away, on the mountain, where men and women are no longer men and women and so no good to us anyway, we are here without anything.

In nothing then we can find Alice, now so far away that I can't bear it but I will see her soon before I die, like the village idiot in the Kingdom of Stones, not Kalfour but one of its antecedents, underneath the world.

Nothing makes my head ache and my heart fear, for if she should come without my reason then what good is it, who will I name her and what callus can make my hand carry her to the music, or bend the light to the tomb of our embrace, now arrogant and unstyled, now melodious, now an atrophy of my kingdom, who is Kalfour, but so alone:

In nothing we can find woman, that light under harbor easy and strange, able and Erda-like in the balm of that ease, limpid and bearing help to black things, rich and weary:

So, I will say it:

[a magic word]

and though it does not all come crashing down my men and the boy our ship, before the Gate to the demesne of the Lemur King, still it is close, bearing eastward, in our turn of the ship down into the burial ground, spinning in the water, our men and my boy and our ship now wearying ourselves into a cascadant thought, shimmering under our skin, trembling as Ulysses before the sound of the sirens, still underneath the water, but surfacing:

We are surfacing beneath the water, under Madagascar, a name for an island with no name, since Marco Polo mistranslated the Arabic and took it for Mogadishu.

Under the water bright my men bear me, a sacrifice, to the mouth of the natives, their bright and searing eyes shining through the water:

I hear you, Alice, under my head, whose name is my own, who bears me like myself, from before I am born, and if I come to die with you it is good, since dying is good, and because all of my children are with me, to be buried with you, like Atlas under a failing Earth, to watch the sky become the sea, at last.

I see her falling around me, princess Alice, the suborned one, sent to the triumph of it, the apportioner, in her magnitude and grace, doomed but bearing witness to the quality of it, as she scoops out the food for the King of Lemurs.

"What a place," I say.

The Lemur King watches me, his yellow eyes bright and wide.

His men are eating and so I ask: "May my men eat?" And the king looks to a space of coral where bowls have been laid out and my men go to them gratefully.

The boy stays, holding my hand.

"Go eat," I tell him, but he will not.

I eat myself then, to remind myself how good it is to endure despite the ridiculous evils that live inside your breast.

It's round and arrogant, a sun, burgeoning, whose mission is unknown to me, but the fire is waxing to bear me too, to where it is going.

"How does it taste?" I ask the boy, and he nods.

The death is far away, like a nearby ridge, shining with light.

Who holds the night over you, centered around the spoonful of my food, bearing eastward, covering my mouth with steam and heat and the seeds of the forest, whose earth rhymes beneath my feet; even though you are immediately beneath me, Alice, still I look for you, because my feet are not my hands, and when I reach for you, you're not there:

"Is she the woman you're looking for?" the Lemur King asks.

And when he asks she's gone. We both look at the space she occupied a moment before.

30.

In flight and under the bent arrow of my regard, my regard who is impertinent, uproarious,
not here nor there, but inside, beating my fist
into my gut, insisting I'm not right, and there is
no corridor here nor emptiness, only the will of
its sound, humming the low music of my urgent
need, to find this ridiculous woman, this nebu-
lous woman, tremulous and searing, stirring the
wait and rot, the faint crock and spot of the meal
and the mull to hear her sounds, shaking the roof,
with her broom in her hand, under the thatch,
making the hiss and howl of the galaxy around
the village scrape the burial ground shape the
naming of her heart, burnt amber umber and re-
covery, to my house:

Now my house is with me, flickering, bowed
but carrying the hate and regard of my regard,
delirious now but strong, flashing night over my
drop, out and up to the wax doll of her spite:

She's a statue here, in grey and chalk, silent under the weight of the night, faintly gleaming and I
touch her cheek and she looks at me, naiad, dry-
ad, woman wood and stone, now determined, to
tell me what I had overlooked:

"What is it?"

She looks up.

"I can't see anything!"

She points.

The Earth is spinning in space.

31.

Some kinds of hell can't be described, not because they are beyond our experience but because they're too intimate. So just imagine the worst thing, not all at once, but slow and over time, the worst thing of yours, which will not leave, and take that with you into the space between me and you, so we can understand each other when I say that hell is with me now, here in my city, my city who is nameless like I am, and from whom I must escape but cannot yet, and whose children are firing into my brain their urgent messages, about all the things I have forgotten:

The thing of it is in part the sound of it, because Alice is a sound, shaken under the boots and kept right out of reach, demanding I be aware of it, and not able to deal with it, but needing to, whose absence shakes my hair and eyes and curls my lips, laughing lunatic to the name of the night and sky who will not demand of me that I see you, though I need to. Why won't the sky demand it? It could; it should; but will not, and I won't either, can't fire it, furl it or find it, it's all gone, but still sounding right out of reach, music from another world.

32.

The right to bacon, to fruit, to disease, to weather, to nutrients, somnolence, arrogance, puissance, fear: shepherded over the mostly empty street detritus of the forge spin in the air feet on sidewalk under the ominous weight of early morning traffic stuck in grooves incalculably vast; I wear my hair wet under my hat, squinting against the light, and the despair of my fellow citizens, looking for the reasoning behind the marionette march taken out and gone over, shaken into a dance, blinking the light, and turning the dial tighter:

As always, the light itself is my liberation, whose story redeems all stories I know, its winter a sojourn from a past inaccessible but still felt, liquid and nowhere to be mandated, the barge in the heat of madness, gaining weight, gaining fervor, sustenance and reward, galleon of starvation and bedtime, who shall turn me down in the night beneath the white sky, gray mask and mast of my fleet so barren to me that I must sing these lines under its pale regard, musician to countenances invisible, gods or judges or gourmands, gimps and griffins, gesturing into the tomb of our last and noble dark:

The right to breakfast. The right to eat, and glare. The right to feel pity, and swear. The right to bury my love.

Not too deep. Just a few inches under. So I can hear her breathing.

33.

The right to a sound meal. The right to lone-liness. The right to grief, and reward, and elegies, elegies coming out of every pore, elegies for each year of your youth, each month, each day and hours, each look you thought was yours alone but was in fact shared, stolen, deprived, codeter-mined, written under you.

If I work to relate the cause and calorie count of my order to you, if I work to release the bur-den of my surmise and its patient and perverse harmonies who will not end me or leave me, if I make the mask of the earth mine, burial mask, all of it mine, in my death:

This is my death, whose art will not be de-prived, nor mentioned in any documents, and will not be written. Because my death is not writ-ten, nor will it be, I can still be alive.

I am always looking for Alice; and have always found her.

But this particular codeterminant in my work also implies that I will not be able to find her, since I still search for her.

The right to a mediocre day. The right to sleep, and silence. The right to grief, and elegies. Elegies come out of every pore because they are what is most required of us now, to grieve for everything that was, and though there is danger in it, like for the Jews, that we should become a religion of sadness, let us not become a religion, only this habit, peculiar but noble, bent to this work:

Alice is at Stanford, working on her dissertation.

I am withdrawing from drugs. Though I fear the drug is not the chemical variety, that is, not external to myself, but one my body is manufacturing on its own.

Chemical Boy.

Chemical Girl.

Dissertate with me on the nature of existence. Get high with me. These are my neurochemicals:

Now colored purple as murex, now ushered under the grief of Caesar, now under Madagascar:

34.

"Did you imagine that you would find your woman here? I keep few, and they are lemurs. But you are wise to have come. And I will give you gifts, because I am king," the Lemur said.

Mogadishu means "holy." So too with lemurs.

We can imagine that the act of delay is itself the nature of desire: even as the star longs to join with its neighbor and form a singularity, but will not, cannot, not yet, so desire is pure only in its unfulfillment, or its coming to fulfillment, not yet.

Not yet. Dear Lord, make me celibate, but not yet. Find me my Alice; but not yet.

Not yet the truth, who hurts me, not yet the birth, who changes me, not yet the starry night in my dark corner of the city, not yet shopping nor sleep, but give me the mystery in its song, howling the waste, howling.

Howl me north, I say, and book a train ticket to see her, though we have promised one another time alone.

How many times have I done this?

Each time I do it I become more fully myself. I am bitter and aged, and as I plunge the knife into her breast, again, I become more fully a killer, plunge myself into her, again, I become more fully her lover, but not yet:

Not yet will I be granted the prize, because it is

sweeter to deny yourself, and because of so many reasons I don't understand.

California is brown and bent down, hiding from the sun, and I am running north on the train, in air conditioning and even wifi, absurdly decadent, waiting for it all to end:

Not yet. The elegy says: it's coming again. This grief you grieve is come again, and coming again: you sing it not only to escape it but to welcome it back: it is yours.

We're waiting, waiting for the war to start.

Each war is like the battle between the sexes: slow and long and brutal, cut mixed and incoherent, both unrelatable and related unceasingly, a wyvern caught in a ball of string, and writhing, writing to be free, but who will never be free because then he would stop, she would cease, to be wyvern.

Knight Parsifal forgets he is Knight Parsifal and man forgets he is man and woman forgets she is woman as they become each other, on the battlefield of love.

No testament is too long, no journey more unfulfilling, uproarious, blessed, a sham, shamrock and mud, mildew and ghosts, reeds, marches, setting suns, a thousand, trillion years, magnets and stars, oceans, regret, the woman writing a letter and never receiving a reply, and the man who can no longer remember how to write.

We are waiting for it to start.

Fire the shot.

Fire the shot, at the right head.

Come, anarchist, for the king awaits your hand, your glorious hand, glowing with glory, set to the match and lock and fire:

35.

Punt what you're not ready for; it's what I do. Kick the can down the road and see how far you can make it go, one foot after another. Left, right, left, hay foot, straw foot, hay foot, straw foot:

Because the immensity of love is its own logic, one ultimately inaccessible to reason, reconciliation, or even narrative, it doesn't really matter what you do to try to explain it, only that you're moving towards it, under its diaphanous shadow, the shadow cast by a camera filter who describes the movement of the mind into love's corridor, indeed, the tunnel of love, sarcophagal, magnificent and weary, supersaturated or grayboned and half-dead, beating the heart, moving the eyes to see who we have become:

I am at sea again. Sans sailors.

We can imagine that the pursuit of love, in its magnificence, provides the gates needed for the story to happen, not only this one—this one hardly even exists—but all the stories surrounding this one.

The maid who knew me as a child and her dead lover, the checkout girl and the dog she kept under her hat, who would whisper to her in English, the Indian conqueror who fell in love with the color red, and had a ceremony devoting himself to it, before every other lover. The city gate who was alive, and saw everything, and the beggar who was, of course, the king, but who unlike most kings never took off the costume to let everyone know it.

The rats and their stories, arching over highways and under barns, under pillows and beds, in hallways, and even starships.

The gates must needs arrive, curtains for the Fall.

Wrap me in the curtains of the Fall, for I am weary of it, and would like to be carried the rest of the way, towards the shining sun and its horrible glory.

The sea, the train, the stars, each hour, my body, my endurance and emolument before the grace of these gods, so to preserve the gates and keep traffic moving, baby.

Keep moving, buddy, this is romance and we've got places to get to.

36.

Keep moving, buddy, this is hay foot, straw foot, hay foot straw foot, stroke, stroke, stroke, stroke.

Stroke.

Stroke.

Stroke.

Stroke.

Stroke the body. Stroke the water. Stroke the paper.

This is how we keep moving, over and over, on the journey of love, always implausible and superstitious, always mad, a luxury without limit, a nightmare without end, it's:

Stroke

Stroke

Stroke

Bear left

Watch your water

Eat at Joe's

And remember, remember the light at your back

As though you were a solar sail, pushing towards Orion:

37.

Gavrilo Princip is my name; let us say it is my name and that we mean what we say when we say Gavrilo Princip, he who met the Black King of Kalfour and was changed forever, in Sarajevo.

Sarajevo from *caravanserai*, from Persian karwan-sarai, "palace, mansion, inn," from Iranian *thraya, "to protect," from the Proto-Indo-European root *tere : "cross over, pass through, overcome."

Pass through, over, and overcome, Gavrilo, for we are shining behind you, lights in the sea:

38.

Gavrilo Princip is my name and this is what we've become;
I am here again;
Again;
I am here again;
Again;
Here I am again;
Black as a steed;
Ready as his mane;
Ominous and weary; your own
This is your own tenor
Sing it right
This is your own tenor
Sing it right, senor,
Here we go
Where we go
Is World War One
In Sarajevo
Land of the caravanserai
Jews or Arabs or Improbably Neanderthals
Come under the influence of the stars and in influenza bear our message down to bear us and its deeds:
Well, what can you say, right?
It's Gavrilo Princip

That guy who shot the Archduke Ferdinand and started the war to end all wars.

But it must be appropriate since all being fair in love and war, and this perverse tale of mine feeling like the love to end all thought of love, I am Gavrilo Princip, with my handgun, loaded and cocked, looking for the man in the plumed hat, so I can fuck up my destiny, just right:

This is your tenor

This is Gavrilo Princip

Sucked into the maelstrom of life, and bent to reward under his gun, knife and axe and weight and head, heady famous fearful light, bent under the weight of that light, to fire:

How many loves begin in war, and why is that?

The panties start dropping when the guns unload.

Men trapped in the ordure of their nature, bent to struggle with brothers who knew, too, that it was coming, and that the masters were ready to die:

And so too, my masters must be ready to die, and I raise my hand, to you, my masters, I will hit you in the throat:

Fire

and Fire

and Fire again

[the Archduke Ferdinand is hit]

A touch, I do confess, a touch.
Touché, mon amour, and now I can hear the
guns, they're firing, they're firing, my love.

They're firing.
Again
and Again
and Again

Stroke

Stroke

Stroke

Stroke

This is my journey and this is my reward
There will be no other agency
I am determined that this be it, you bitch.
Alice,
Do you see the blood on your hands?
We're killing the Duke again:

(Cut off his head)

[I hold the Archduke's dead]

39.

But one death is not enough and we shall have more.

40.

But not yet. We can always re-fight World War One. So what if I stick Gavrilo Princip's ghost into my spine to rummage around and look for treasure; he's there anyway. He'll be there again, still arrogant and peaceful, noble and unsatisfied, still looking for the answer.

In many ways Alice is Co-Terminant with Wonderland, her edges its edges and her empires its, even if they be not the same thing, perhaps she contains it, or it her, or, as in a long and uninterrupted love affair, they merely occupy the same place at the same time.

Because Alice's curves are the curves of its tunnels, and its madness hers also, and the redemption, what Wonderland offers, is hers too.

What is the redemption of woman?

Who is she selling, right over the edge? What curve of space occupies her thought, turbulent and uprising storm, the nadir of the earth and the opening of the sky, cold sky canyon vessel uprooted and spinning, bare earth, water and round maw of sound and rain:

Redemption because she brings you back in, man.

When you thought you were out, she pulls you back in.

So woman is a kind of mafia, and wonderland its ultimate expression.

I am heading north.

She is in San Francisco.

Call Alice. I think she'll know, When logic and proportion have fallen sloppy dead, and we shall revive them, we the necromancers under your basement, we revive them, for the Main Event, now featuring in Barnum and Bailey's, the Great American Show, whose lights do not end, and whose voices do not soften, and whose majesty rings the night, the eternal and canyoned night, canyons deeper than any in Los Angeles or Arizona, deeper than any Hebrew or Templar temple, underneath the order of the soul the permanent midnight daydream describes its reasons for the curtain and their management, breaking a leg, over and over and over:

"We have hot dogs, pizza, chips, and other health foods in the dining car at the rear of the train," the conductor says over the intercom, and I wonder how deep I have to go to get me and Alice out of here, and what it would mean.

This is also hell, you understand. That hell is simply a hole in the ground. Where you can be redeemed.

41.

Each limitless codeterminant of an arc of descent of an artillery round—the human bodies, soldiers and other passerby in the late medieval volta—they bend like I do for Alice to describe the shape of the storm, as a bird the thermal, or a turtle the Gulf Stream, burying below the earth the ritual of the hidden logics of battle, not the beat-down but the movement into its exact description, like a military photograph in impossible geometries mid assault, charting missiles, movements and plans of the ordnance and armies thrust through the night and mud to gut the heart of history out of its comfortable ribcage and plop it into the scientist's table:

This is my heart, doctor.

Tell me: what is it I've done?

What torsional limit, not of the human body, but the brain, describes the rendition of Man down into his basement in Wonderland?

I fear that is what this document has become, perhaps was designed to be. That torture is not only the mere indulgence of sadists, but also the measure of the captive: to see what it is he can become.

The Black King is not far away; for he wants victory too, even as I do. To see what it is I am and will be.

Who is the thing? And what shape. What

tricks does he perform, and, even, what revelations will this experiment uncover, of our sacrifice to god and heaven, science, and Wonderland?

Who is my thing in Wonderland uttering the names of the ghosts, saying my mantra and my mission saying my thing, so here I am, radiant, in glory, your slave:

42.

The meaning of life, the universe and every-thing.

Bent to, and willing, I am a bullet, hereafter and not far, my righteous legions, my golden hel-met, my shotgun ass, saltpeter sulfur and spark, hellion heal me for I impair and decline over my short arc, zero in, my heart, my head and dart, for we war with one another, as brothers dance in the shtetl ear to ear, beard to beard, with my knife at your back.

Come to my knife at your back, brother, for my love is terrible and I will have you, I will have you closer in.

Fire

Fire

Fire

Fire

Fire

and fire

inconstant angel, smearing your light over the trench

fire me to read the names of the dead

we are rising over the mast of heaven

Tommy
Hear me Tommy
For I am fallen
Under the spell of the light
This is my wisdom from the lord
Who is the ground beneath your feet
Don't get up Tommy
They're shooting at you
Don't get up Tommy.
Princip hears you too, Tommy.

43.

I assert the conditions of my enslavement; not to escape, as I no longer believe that to be possible, but to control the conditions of my prison.

This is my heart, and these the wires, this the agency who hires me for the job, warbling from their colored modern mast, spirographic barber pole cum airship buoy, magnanimously declaring that I may remain employed, enslaved, and here are the coordinates and here the password, for my foray into the land, over the arch of the city, airport, and bust, navigating the earthworks of flight patterns, huge stanzas as cold fronts descending over the plane, blinking my moniker, reminding me of my name, my name is ( ) and I am yours, here to fire and wait, always:

It is also becoming more likely that I have misunderstood the nature of you, my interlocutor. I realize now it was comforting for me to believe that you had been liberated, were from either some prior or future time free from the crevasses my masters have placed me in, but no, I see that isn't right.

We're here together.

The horror of democracy is the horror of language; or freedom to describe our surroundings equal in power to our ability to manufacture them, and prescribe their order, all together, in the cave, debating:

Where has she gone?

Hunting, in San Francisco. For gazelles.

But are you my peer or are you . . . well. What does the word even mean? And how many translations systems will this have been through, before it reaches you—first and foremost through my own brain!

Of course I must imagine you too. They do not tell me who is receiving these broadcasts. If they even know.

You are a woman, sunburnt and drinking from a cold metal ewer in Arizona, waiting for the mail to arrive.

You are an interdimensional alien, monitoring the frequencies known to populate this region of space, so as to make a study for a learned journal; your first monograph.

You are a child, playing with a wooden block, chewing on it like a dog, unable to understand the meaning of the words I speak, but knowing the import of their tone, instinctively.

You are dying in hospital. Anything to keep death at bay—any story at all, is welcome, no matter how bad.

You are my masters, sadists who enjoy watching the "exceptions" come to know their prison before you squash them out, my masters who know too that they need me, their voice, to both enforce the limits of their prison and to help them understand it themselves, something they cannot do without help.

You are crows, firing flight black dark over the wind to food.

Hear me, crows, for I have met the Black King of Kalfour, and he sends word:

44.

I've never flown into orbit before. Where the gangway meets the place we can see out over the terminal—dark grey clouds gather rain over the huge red lights of the control tower. Steel antennae extend twenty meters out from its bulbous head like threatening spines. The flight attendant smiles at me and then speaks into her radio.

I've been given a seat by the window and so can watch the workmen load our luggage with their huge, mechanical cranes.

They wear bright green, and drive between glowing red cones.

The cabin is filling with oxygen and I feel sleepy. When I first entered the craft the air smelled strange—some aerosol drug they use to keep us calm.

A huge man is seated next to me and I have to shift sideways so I can continue to write. They bring him a harness extension to fit around his big gut.

The cabin fills with blue light. "Check valves"—a voice over the radio. The fans turn on full speed and we all ease back into our seats as the oxygen hits us.

Our screens light up with a propaganda presentation hosted by a vaguely Nazi-looking woman with a very high voice and an extremely tight bun in her hair.

They fire the rockets then and our harnesses contract. The craft trembles and I watch the heat-shielded geodesics of the terminal shiver behind the steam.

The blue lights glow brighter, and the mechanized loaders retract their skinny arms, retreating into the steam.

Then a huge whine and a low, ominous sound like drums, and I realize we are already airborne.

Down below, the city is the most peaceful I've ever seen it, drifting away beneath us, like my life.

The blue bulbs burn even brighter and it is as though we're underwater, and in some queer reversal the Earth spins amidst a watery ocean of space.

After the first burn our harnesses relax and they offer us entertainment and beverages. But I only want to stare down below, at the canyons of sky insurmountable over the earth.

- -

They tell me she has been assigned as translator to a semi-permanent orbital installation to negotiate the terms of one of the new communiqués with our masters.

Alice has fallen up, into the music of space, whose sound has no end, whose urgency is itself mammalian, leaping into the void to scream:

- -

All at once I'm filled with a longing for home,

even though it is a place I've never been.

The clouds whorl like cream. Almost I believe I can escape. Perhaps this is it—already escaping, however briefly. Some deep knowledge of the end of the earth—not an eschatos, just an ordinary death—lurks underneath my ears and on my chin, to teach me who I have been.

The Earth is so dark—I realize that now—just a black space rock.

There's a new kind of nihilism in the flight attendant's smile, one I've not seen before. As though she knows some terrible secret she mustn't reveal to us. But I'm also tired—perhaps I'm hallucinating.

At first it seemed strange to me that so many writers would be visited with hallucinations but it no longer does. In my experience, it's true of at least half of us.

Whether only those so "blessed" turn to writing, or whether writing is instead what triggers the hallucinations I can't say. Perhaps it is both.

('Hallucination,' of course, is not quite the right word, but then, there is so little proper language for what we do.)

Although I find it increasingly difficult to describe accurately—it becomes more difficult, not less, with each attempt—still I suspect it is important to do it if you and I are to understand what has happened to me and Alice.

It is tempting to draw a picture like the one drawn for the original Alice: that her hallucinations were triggered by a particular place, of Wonderland and its environs. I know that this is not ultimately the most powerful explanation but I must begin somewhere.

People like to write about the spirits of places: as though they are possessed of their own weight and breadth, even consciousness. As though a place were a Mind whose reaches we encounter when we step into it. Moving that metaphor one step further, then, we could say animals and plants, both mobile and immobile, being also possessed of minds, move through these greater minds as plankton through a region of the sea.

All of this is, of course, quite "normal"—a version of the world as many of us experience it.

(I'm sorry, the large man to my left has fallen asleep and his gut has swelled, pressing me into the wall of the cabin, so I am finding it difficult to concentrate. If my handwriting becomes difficult at this point I do apologize.)

So, the problem arises when we attempt to understand what is 'aberrational' in the nature of hallucination. Like so many phenomena, its ultimate cause may well be beyond us, but we can, if we work at it, grow closer to understanding the nature of its operation.

Always the problem arises: whenever I begin

to speak of this I remember quickly how the nature of the this inquiry threatens to turn itself into a philosophical disquisition of some length. So, if you feel an apology is necessary for such endeavors, I cheerfully make one, and if you would like to skip ahead to the next chapter, where I dock with the orbital station, and encounter my Alice once again, please do so—I cannot be offended at this point since I am only words on paper!

But one thing is clear to many people: insanity vs. sanity, normal vs. abnormal, hallucination vs. "standard" perception, all of these binaries are dependent chiefly on an agreement, a social contract, which is mediated as we have come to understand it, chiefly through language.

Wiser men than me have opined how language itself can determine what kind of reality we are able to perceive. I make no claims as to that, but I do know that it is extremely difficult to narrate a story which has happened to you and you alone. That is, a story in which you encounter phenomena either very rare in human experience, or, perhaps, entirely unknown.

Still, humans would not have survived for very long if we did not have some way of accounting for new phenomena—and this we do chiefly through language—it is our method of error checking. But observe too: words alone are not enough. You must also have authority—if only a little—if you are to be believed; even listened to. We can all imagine how the cry of 'wolf!' would be heeded coming more quickly from an elder than from a lackadaisical child.

Still, when we speak of hallucination, our work is further complicated because we are dealing with interior phenomena. Experiences that happen only within. (Although I have ultimately determined that this is not, quite, true).

Here in modern times, one thinks immediately of psychoanalysis, which has been popularized in at least two dominant, interrelated forms: "the talking cure," and drugs. Often we think of talk therapy as way for the "victim" (although already the language is wrong) of hallucination to "feel better" about their "trauma" (I do not dispute that hallucination can be traumatic; still, that is not their primary characteristic).

Drugs perform a similar function: it is hoped that the "patient" (again, wrong word!) will either have these abnormal phenomena diminished or at least reduced.

Again, men and women far wiser than I have written of the chief drawback to these two modes of treating hallucination: both ignore the social character of perception. At least with the "talking cure," we assume, society is present: 'doctor' (whose name, creepily enough, derives from words meaning 'to make appear right') and 'patient,' are 'in society' together, after all. But this ignores the reality of the situation. In the talking cure, there is never any discussion—any serious discussion—of whether the 'wolf' was real or not. That the wolf was false has already been assumed, and the 'patient' must, instead, talk of their feelings, about how it 'felt' to 'cry wolf' and so on.

And with drugs, of course, it is hoped, that pharmacologically, the 'patient' will be incapable of ever seeing wolves again!

So: we know the drawback. A major alternative, not surprisingly, comes from premodern societies in the form of the shaman. The shaman's job, after all, is to hallucinate: to journey into realms few others in the tribe dare to enter: foreign realms of the mind and spirit—or if not foreign, then so deep and forgotten by everyday experience as to be unfamiliar.

Already we are coming into a clearer picture of the problem when we speak of hallucination: that both psychoanalysis and pharmacology remain mostly on the surface. They remain afraid of what is underneath. (Even though both claim, of course, to be dealing with 'depth': 'hidden' feelings, and 'secret' operations of biochemicals and the like).

When we are dealing with hallucination we are dealing with storytelling: what is the story? What knowledge does it contain?

And let us not make the mistake of concluding that our imaginary shaman here, belongs to some 'pure' 'ur-praxis' or original method, now lost to us. It is easy to see how the 'treatment' of the shaman could be just as conservative: you were visited, the shaman will tell you, by such and such a god, or spirit, and if you propitiate that god your unwellness will leave you. Here again we can see a certain hesitancy to deal with hallucination itself: rather than deal with the specifics of its nature our imagined shaman seeks instead to fit your abnormal or unusual experience into an existing pantheon of gods and spirit relations—an oeuvre which is doubtless very complex and provides a kind of narrative relief: you can find a place in the story, after all.

But consider the nature of these kind of stories: Zeus chasing women who turn into trees and cows, Krishna leading magical armies across fantastic landscapes to win the heart of some many-armed monster-woman, invisible devils or djinn who care deeply about everything that happens on Earth and just can't stop fucking with us—stories all packed with detail and delight and full of ethnographic information (Krishna is blue, for instance, because he grew out of a blue mushroom cult)—but again, we are not dealing with the nature of hallucination. At root, hallucination is this: a new story. New knowledge. And what we do with it is entirely up to us. Because our ability to absorb these new stories and new knowledge into our culture so often depends on the charisma, authority (and stubbornness!) of the person who had the hallucination, I see it is my duty to offer some advice in the event such a hallucination should happen to you. I know, probably it is true that I too am avoiding the nature of hallucination, the same as the shrink, and the doc, and the shaman . . . perhaps I will never get there. But in the event my advice is, perhaps, a little different, it may still have some worth:

First: decide if you really want to deal with the character of your hallucination. There is no shame in sidestepping it. If you gain relief from therapy, or drugs, or religious solutions, of course I am happy for you and wish you well.

My advice then, is for the other group: likely you have already begun to write. If not, you will soon start.

And it is here that our work really begins. The building of knowledge does happen through writing—though not exclusively, it is still one of our chief methods.

That you are visited by phenomena unknown to us must be treated as a blessing: only you have been provided with this key.

And unlike the terrible gatekeeper in Kafka's castle, who provides a unique door, only for you, only to shut it in your face, this door has no guardian but you. Only you may open it. (And Aldous Huxley notwithstanding, you needn't use hallucinogens to do it either).

To understand—to attempt to understand—hallucination, is to attempt to understand narrative.

Or, to put it more immediately, it is to tell stories.

Perhaps we are all trapped in our private hallucination, and only language offers any escape.

Let me speak, briefly then, of my own hallucinations. Yes, Mr. Beckett, I will fail better, I promise, and here I will fail again.

I was visited by malevolent gods some years previous. These gods attempted to destroy my personality, as well as my body. The extent to which my society cooperated in this attempted destruction (using the methods previously described: talk therapy, pharmacology, and religion) is the extent to which my subsequent life has been characterized by a certain paranoia towards my fellow man (an experience, I know, not uncommon with my fellow writers).

In life, as in fiction, one has to make do with what one has at hand. Heroes in stories go on quests for sacred objects, build new alliances, fight wars, fall in love, bear children, and perform sacrifices to do battle with malevolent gods. What

I did was begin to write.

Narrative is the most powerful weapon human beings possess, and it is both closely guarded and accessible, by birthright, to all life.

All in the execution, as they say. Malevolent gods have many more weapons than we do. And I suspect that the use of my weapon—writing—results not in the injury, or destruction of my supernatural enemies, but rather a reluctant peace-process, a coming to know one another through battle—which is, after all, what war is. The ultimate flirtation.

My decision—one I cannot necessarily recommend but which I nevertheless offer freely, was to always return to a point of trust in the veracity of my hallucinations. In this way, I have continued to learn about them, and as I continue my trial beneath the arms of my masters, and look for Alice, I can say that this trust has proven useful.

45.

Some kind of light rock Muzak penetrates the cabin as our ship reorganizes itself for arrival, splitting us passengers in-harness into independent docking units: pods to attach to the station for our journey through customs.

The station looks like a huge, bulbous spider with multicolored eyes. Under one of the large orange "eyes" my pod slips into the gantry's hand, which turns me into the airlock, passing under the flickering lights of the station, and the unblinking stars behind them.

- -

A mother tongue is like this station: unsleeping, slow, and calm. It awaits an ocean, behind us, to wash over us.

Whoosh.

- -

Whosoever breaks a tie must replace it, but I cannot. I can just barely function with the work I have to do, of finding Alice. Or, more accurately, finding myself, in relation to her. I have begun to suspect that Alice may not, actually, want to be found.

Still, I must find her anyway. I know better than her the perils of this place.

- -

I'm reviewing her qualities
Reminiscing over the things I've seen

Snatches of conversation
A dirty word
Like a gleaming pearl
In her mouth
- -

So close yet so far in the West, and having giv-
en the reason to it we melt away, unable to see or
know what it is we've done, who we've become.

Become, of course, the landowners and lords
from whom we'd fled.

So already we are dead, but the name remains,
and the idea, of the west, and since it has no longer any bearing on reality the story moves further
and further away from us, into legend, necro-
mancy, Tartarus, and dreams.

The American Dream is a western dream, now
a low and intimate nightmare, promising all the
things we cannot have.

I cannot have Alice and so I am inseparably
bonded both to her and the cities of America—
whatever has happened to them, they may all be
gone by now, as Alice has—underneath her cheek
and to hear the music of her words and peer into
the darkness around her neck.
- -

To kill a rich man is a great joy, for without it
there is nothing. Their evil is of no concern: like
the moon, it will return. But their bodies rot in
the ground.

\- -

We shall burn Brooklyn and it shall be a better city than it was standing. It will be a holy temple of black ash.

46.

The description of Alice's interrogation of me at the space station will have to wait—I do not have the energy for it now. I find her a very tedious woman, but I am in love with her.

I have taken a vacation at my family's plot of land east of the Cascades, in Washington State. Here we do not do very much and I can pretend I am John Steinbeck working on another Great Western Novel rather than a freak who has been blackmailed into perverse and non-sensical adventures by invisible aliens.

Still, I am able to do perhaps a reasonable facsimile of Steinbeck: I offer catchy aphorisms which explore the Fate of Man (grim) and the Role of Woman in Society (unknown) and the Nature of the Cosmos (also unknown, but intriguingly formed from a Greek word for "a woman's dress.")

One day is much the same as another here: breakfast, lunch and dinner, cooked by us all and eaten with great gusto, before we retire for naps. If I were not deathly afraid of being kidnapped again at any moment, I would be enjoying myself without reservation. But then, the question arises: are these kidnappings, truly? I thought I was on a noble quest to rescue my beloved. Is it possible I have come to regard that, too, as a tedious chore?

No, not exactly. That also would be too simple and would ignore the love, which is annoying but real.

Still, they are kidnappings, you see. I am not entirely in control of where I go; I am being led.

What is the nature of the Muse? Steinbeck would know. I do not. But both of us are bound to her seal.

- -

Of course, to search for a woman is to search for yourself. I, at the end of a long line of generations infected with self-help books find it difficult to discuss this without irony. Still I feel I must discuss it. Please feel free to skip ahead to the next chapter if you wish. Although, as I have already broken my last promise I had best not make another about what you will find there.

What does it mean to search for yourself, and what are you likely to find there. Rapidly you find other people. For me, an insincere but loving father and a devoted, simple-minded mother. Some lovers, bright and stern and, all of them, readers.

What have I learned already, doctor?

Oh, my dear boy, I see a neurosis. Now merely channel Philip Roth and you will have these aliens off your back in a jiffy. They hate neuroses, I can tell you.

Readers, of night and day. The light, and its burdens, over the page, behind the page. Melancholy isolationists boldly captured in stark photographs in museum expositions—you've seen them—strapped into their iron chair contemplating the manuscript before them.

A search for searchers. Like some terrible remake of a John Wayne film cast with New York socialites and gay queens, having orgies in the desert.

But also, nothing lonelier.

The scout for scouts.

Prefacer to prefaces.

Pre-genesis.

She is out there and I must find her, but only because I barely exist. If I existed, I would already have a woman, already be bound by her and by the dynamics of our physical affair, and the lesion of it: scar in time. But I do not, and have none, and Alice is calling, behind the winter-screen of this country hillside, calling my name.

So, we can't be sure what is happening, least of all I.

It is not enough to declare a direction, give yourself a name, arm and gird yourself, sing, dance, scribble and perform—although perform perhaps comes closest.

As we echo the world perhaps it becomes clearer to us. And our charade, though it remains just as mysterious, acquires purpose: to unravel the game in which we have been laid, and make our own.

Alice, you seem more invisible to me than

ever. Why did you come with me into this abyss?

- -

No flashing light will tell the truth for Alice—
no grave wind nor circumpolar galaxy can uplift
us from this nadir: it is all-reaching, a dark epiph-
any, mother or father, twin, patient devil and lover bent on serving us into destruction.

For as we go in there being no appropriate
words we either develop new vocabulary or decide not to speak of it . . .

"What brings you to Wonderland?"

"You, Alice."

"Ha, well that's only my name. This isn't my
Wonderland."

"I know. We're married, you and I. You've forgotten."

"I fear you've mistaken me for someone else.
Are you a courier? A magician? A diplomat, perhaps? I can't let you enter without the proper pa-
perwork, you know."

- -

I have been placed in solitary confinement,
although the space is well lit and features a simulated aural and visual scape of an ocean through
the porthole.

I can do nothing—but what troubles me is
that this does not seem to bother me.

Again I am Parsifal, and though I still remember my name I have forgotten my quest, and this

gives me an exquisite pleasure, akin to the student's who has long ago given up asking any questions.

It seems I am just along for the ride.

The porthole is programmable and I've switched it to a dry Western forest, complete with the distant whine of a highway and a glorious multitude of birdsong.

Perhaps there is some similarity between being a prisoner in a simulated reality in an alien universe and being alone in a distant and silent forest: in each, one is faced head-on with one's own thoughts. Nature, either cruel and indifferent or beautiful and mysterious, is a mirror for the self.

The knowledge that I must escape fills me with foreboding—a black pit in my stomach. The trees seem to understand this and as the wind sets them swaying they lean in to listen.

Why has Alice come to Wonderland? I could claim it was the Black King's doing but I know it isn't. She wants to be here. I press the green intercom button but no one answers.

- -

The hillside view has rotated outside the porthole so I am afforded a beautiful view down into a mountain meadow, where a deer is half-hidden in the tall grass, busy munching on her dinner.

I say hello to the deer but she ignores me—she

is, after all, only a computer simulation.

The light has a dreamlike quality, slowly moving the forest into yellow ash.

Who am I to have been bereaved here, shrunken and solemn under these failing lights, as thought of honor or direction, only a slow and creeping malaise, like happiness, hacking its way into my senses with a fine-toothed saw, making entry points my soul, illumining the pawed and powder paltry humans encased within myself, such a grotesque menagerie as we all keep inside but are content most always to leave invisible and unexamined.

The deer appears quite intelligent and is staring at me fixedly, as though possessed of a terrible secret, like Alice has, a burial urn of an idea, sleepy fire not yet palpable but seen, just at the edge, a wave of dark water bubbling, leaking over the edge.

The deer has lain down for a nap, and soon I will do so as well, on the heated cot they've provided me.

Far beneath me I can feel the earth, a dark bauble promising me transformation.

47.
How huge is the deafness I find myself in
Unable to see anything
Or hear my words
I am the idiot
Boxed in
And sanding right
The slope of my thoughts
Towards truth and bewilderment
Out under the fading sun I slip into its grace,
Knowing I never needed anything at all.
- -
We won't know the end of it
But I can see it in red
Under the hills
Creeping away from me
Through to the poem
The light has decided to write without me

48.

One of the purposes of the simulation becomes clear to me: that Nature in her raw form is so hypnotic that, to some degree, one's desires come to seem meaningless. Confronted with Nature, you can become the ultimate voyeur, and be subsumed into the life of grass, bird and flower, entirely forgetting your own.

It is no wonder animism was the dominant religion of our ancestors—they must have felt they hardly existed at all.

The whippoorwill and the chickadee and the sparrow take turns announcing themselves, along with the owl and the chipmunk and the deer. It is tempting to believe their innocence is a direct by-product of my presence as a 'colonial power,' but that is too simple.

For one, neither of us is entirely real to the other. Our visit is brief and it is not as though I am a part of their food chain.

So we are allowed to be bonded by simple curiosity.

"Are you ready to begin?" she says.

"Yes."

"Why did you come to Wonderland?"

"To find you."

"But you don't know who I am."

"You're my wife."

"You're hallucinating."

"Maybe, but it is still true within the hallucination."

"How did we meet?"

"On a work detail. I was suffering from heat stroke. You brought me to hospital."

"In reality I've worked here for five years. If I determine you are not dangerous you will be permitted to enter, and we do provide free medical care, if you wish. You could visit one of our therapists."

"We are prisoners of an alien cabal. They want me to sacrifice you as a demonstration of loyalty but I have refused. Because I still love you."

It seemed my words had touched her; she said nothing for a long moment.

"Are you carrying any weapons?"

"No."

"Then welcome aboard Wonderland. I wish you success in all of your ventures."

"Including regarding you?"

"Newcomers often enjoy the Mayberry Bar—we have karaoke and other more advanced simulations. I would like to talk to you further."

"You've never looked more beautiful."

She left then, and I found my door had been opened and fresh clothes laid out. I dressed and entered the space station proper.

49.

On the one hand, it is too easy to get out. My masters have made it perfectly clear all that is required: I could even be permitted to leave with Alice if only I gave up writing.

The writing gives way to hallucination, which gives way to writing. Even more than my masters there is no escape from it, though it provides the luxury of determining the texture of my prison. The latest model simulator: writing.

The documentation process does provide additional burdens. All these are well known of course—writers are terribly self-absorbed little beasts, but chief among them is the Heisenbergian difficulty that observing and writing about a subject changes it.

Even that does not quite do it justice, since it isn't true I can simply write myself wings and Alice in love with me and willing to escape, and have it be so. The obligatory changes are usually more subtle—but subtle or not they are entirely out of my control.

Writing is the red 'change' button, not knowing what the new costume will be.

Yet if I cease to do it, and dip once more into the 'unexamined life,' as it were, then I will never be free.

The karaoke bar in question is hideously garish: huge inflatable pop stars leer monstrously from the corners, bobbling on their helium strings.

Yet the clientele seems unusually serious—such as one might find at a poetry reading or small religious gathering.

The first singer takes the stage and suddenly I am transported: he is a professional voice, and its power washes over me, revealing secrets I did not know were there.

I see Alice then, perched on the far corner of the bar, holding a fluted stem.

The next singer takes the stage and she is just as good—better even—and I wonder whether Wonderland is some kind of secret artist's colony. A place for political exiles, perhaps?

I move and sit next to Alice at the bar. She doesn't look at me. I reach out and touch her hand. She leaves it there for a moment, but then moves it away.

- -

The quality of being alone with your thoughts is a mysterious one: thoughts are like people, and as unpredictable. Or perhaps more like relatives: you know them well enough that they feel like, and indeed are, you.

But there is a quality of visitation to them: here are the thoughts you had not seen for some time and now you are back amongst them, as though you had not left.

It is a blessing. I must make friends with my thoughts, as they are likely to be the only freedom I ever attain. Even if I do bring Alice to freedom, and I with her, this may still be true.

I wish there were more to it—some secret I could ascribe to it, a hidden door whose location I could divulge—perhaps there is and I do not see it.

I find I return continually to the mountain simulation in my thoughts—I am relaxed there, and danger seems not as near. I wonder how much time our ancestors were able to spend simply lounging in a field. They were fortunate men.

I wonder too whether my own story of trial, in being akin to Christian and other narratives of 'testing,' is not somehow masochistic—a desperate attempt to seem relevant in a universe which is ultimately indifferent.

But then, perhaps the old quest and messianic narratives are right, and we are being tested, to be purified into a divine fire.

It may come as a surprise, daffodil or demon, wrought meant and shaped from our dreams, under the bed, under the sun, without light or dark, but numinous: a slow tremor in the hand reminding of the whisk of the sky and the avalanche of the sound of the perturbation in the orbits of these our celestial bodies, so new, so delicate, the undulating river of thought, as writ in Milky Way.

I took her hand again and she did not move it away.

‑ ‑

All winters at night begin within, under the drum of the heavens a bitter order summons your dark to chant the hours, keeping track of the woof and warp who threads your little town: turnip and bellwether, racist or ordinary diseased, the flagship of music, his century sent to learn who it is masks the earning of our fates, still enmeshed but ever more spectacular, starry web enrobing the dark spilling out of you:

We endure the border silence, taking silence within, the silence of conspiracy (all borders are conspiracies, even cell membranes), shaken to root each tribe's spokesman to enact the bearing roof, the tribal baron, who is not a man, woman or child but an effigy, a pidgin mutation who I wear, in my disordered quest through the boundary country yet I am not disordered: I find right the music who led me hear and which I tap under my shoe as the vistas pass over and the mocking Lemur King Loki grins at my imprisonment, earning my weight on the swing out and over the Nothing and silent silk who coats our nightmares, ticking towards the door:

Only pass the door, brother, and step out, pass the door and lean in, set to, shake off and bend

to honor the humble trolls provincial curve of
bridge as we begin, my love, our turning over,
under and through the enactment of the passing
across, within and through:

a rock tossed and shimmering slipping round
under oboe to water, the duck docking time and
shuddering dimples, in your watered cheeks:

- -

It is a wickedness, of course, to leave at all—a
deep and most necessary wickedness without
which we would be dead.

A woman provides such perplexities as to
be ultimately unknowable—yet to come within
reach of being known must be the most frustrat-
ing and enticing thing of all.

- -

We'll clip under the river
Oak and fir
Ferret out the tragedies like ticks
And crush them under fingernail
Each smart of sun a token
Of the years we spent apart

- -

We haven't remembered anything
It isn't one the ticket
No orderly trajectory
Just a burning gas-can
And a feather in your hair
Hoorah hoorah

50.

Invincible Autumn
We don't know another name for it
Rambunctious ludicrous swelling auburn
We can see it coming
A living locomotive
Each suction cup attached as a lifeboat
To the surfacing vessel
Me and Alice
Tartarus and Light
Dimming the lamps for dinner
And trimming the wicks for the long delight
Of the storm
No other winter will change us
But this one
Close but still out of reach
Like her
Invincible Autumn
Storm coming
Black winter sky
Like a warm coat
Under her sheltering hair
No winter but in her
The black forge
Of these emblems:
A chair, bent with a wheel to ease tired feet
And the table
Large enough to feed eleven

Black rubber sandals
And spandex shorts
My beard and hers entangled:
Invincible Autumn
Blackens the sky
Blackens the hands
Reddens the face
And lures the eye under the coals
Promising weight
And love
And the sky
I can see her writing
A letter to the gods
Would that I were one of them
So I could read her words in black ink
And wine.

- -

The grey ash-skirt of the wind
haunts the sky for me
dripping its rhythms over the house
—gauze and sleep—
under the burial keep
We're scraping stones into knives

- -

"How long have you been working here?" I ask
her.

"About a year."

"Is it nice?"

"No, not really."

"I never thought of you as a government agent."

"Come have a drink with me."

Invincible autumn shakes her coat

Over the balcony

Looking for ticks

Checking her lipstick

Stripping the deck

and staining it

Pins in her hair

Moon overhead

Under the silence of the valley

Each bird is a devil with a secret

Each tree a tome of history

Laughing at our antics

Monkeys in the afternoon.

Before lunch.

The lupin are blessings

And the Saint John's Wort is hiding under the grass.

I try to imitate the bird but he flies off

Alice is washing her hair under the tree

Waiting for summer

for the plane to pass over

Around the bend

Where the lights go out

And the birds open their mouths into the dark
Invincible autumn is not a surprise
It's almost a curse
But not quite
It slams you back in
And puts on the music
Warns you about
The beating weight in your brain
And stretches you out on the string
Merry fall weather
Drenched and beating
And with no sleep
Nor thought of any
She is waiting for midnight
To cut off her dress
And turn down the trees
Under the light
Slipping away down into her
To demand the truth
Which order is it
Which hour
Which reason or other
Which home
and which service
Will you perform
In the roll down under
Into dark
Knowing she's waiting
Burning

The midnight dress
Over the midnight stars
Making a midnight halo around her mouth
To drench us in light
- -
No silence will come
For he is already here
True flames
Black ocean
and warts
The stent of the stain of youth
All my own
Burnt well and open
Over the grief of love to you
- -

We lament as though there were discrete long-ings—as though they could be divided—this from the other, the cheap from dear and prized from common, foreign, native and unnameable, each heroic in its majesty, an illustration in full form of a startling array of fantasies—a bazooka to tank your fortunes, settle your middle into a caress with death.

We begin as though each moment were eter-nal and this is wise—the height of wisdom—and yet not conducive to beginnings, which must take time, and need an end.

In one sense, I have no time left. This narrative has already terminated and my contribution into the cosmic bawl-yawp has been categorized, theorized and catalogued by my masters, as though nothing else needed to be said.

But there is so much that needs to be said. I want to say so much.

Alice, be brave for me, if I should turn coward. If I should retreat from this hell without you and either betray us both and flee or die in the attempt to rescue you, be better than me, and more sensible, and make peace with our masters—find out what makes them tick—we will defeat them in time.

Be bold and succor the flame within, who will not turn, his might not black like Blake and hand but white from heat, sent ordered and wrought to bear you over starbound and into the deep ocean under stars, a Mercury shining to home, lunging below and howling, through the bubbles, the riddle we bear through our hands, mouths and teeth, through the sky and its shifting faces and the world below, numerous, numinous portal out from the body and back again: an engine is churning, Alice, of our love, so desperate that it consumes these worlds and I will not answer for the character of its dissolution nor for its slovenly look, enraptured by time and not looking for it— in fact it flees it, sailor with no keel, nor mouth but only a bird, wind-whistle around himself bent on spinning the earth into his hand.

I don't know why I love you, but I do. And this curse is my own to bear, however it works out.

I will riddle you something, my masters:

Why was I one of the ones chosen to be visited with your anarchic glory?

What does it imply that all your tools—or all those you have shown me—have been given over to me?

These are such useless tools, master. Like Cassandra, or Pandora. But at the same time I fear that without them we would not have stories.

Set to in the earth, and hunker, each storm in succession carves the face into glory, and slumber and ache shall spoon breakfast into your mouth, to die in ecstasy.

Let he lumbering come under you, shake you out of your grave and into the wind, where we are watching, where we know the secret—all secrets, and how useless they are—and what to do with it and them, each vessel cloaked in black like one of my names: just starfront poem and cemetery: a denouement, eager for the whipping of it and the lip of the flamed exhaust, firing me into these careful futures.

So careful, Alice. Card Castle Alice. Trampoline Alice, bouncing for joy, to tremble in the light.

What can I say. These powers are worth nothing without you. Less than nothing. Yet I will order them anyway, to see what it is you are, what kind of man, wo-man, and which raft will bear this thing of us out of the kelp bed that's stuck us.

51.

We are not here; we have not arrived. Nor can I bring us here. Here to this cabin.

It is surrounded by woods, and crickets are singing outside. (This sound is said to sound very much like opera when you slow it down).

The doorway into death—he whose reaches order the senses and provide agency for the fruits of the earth—is poetry.

Poetry flings death wide open.

In opening to death, I am trying to bring us here but I can't—my masters do not wish it.

And there is another reason: I fear I no longer know the way out, with or without Alice.

The truism—or is it an aphorism? are all aphorisms truisms?—"down the rabbit hole" with all its attendant meanings of irreversibility suggests that our journey is not one from which you can return.

Still, it is important I try, and that I do it with death, which is poetry.

Death is a kind man and he means well, even if he does not always know what he is about.

"What is it you're doing?" Alice asks.

She has found me studying the controls to the station's weapons systems.

"Where is it that you believe we are?" I ask her.

Is it possible to love wisdom too much? In the quest for a well-balanced life, are we obligated to consume some 'anti-wisdom' as well?

My philosophy will not be the setter-into-motion—only I can be that.

With you, Alice.

Hold my hand.

If we should brake, do not fear me. We are become agents of death, and our horrors are our ticket out.

How long do you think it takes to contemplate atrocity? On the one hand, it is clearly something governments do and have done for years and decades at a time, so much so that governments become a kind of "atrocity management system." On the other, only an instant is enough, and having done so you are immediately catapulted into the fraught philosophical territory of the Nietszchean Superman cum Raskolnikov, trembling on the edge of an ethical abyss.

You become a monster. And in becoming a monster you become deeply and profoundly human. In the most basic sense—and one that would serve well as an epigraph for our species—humans are beings who commit atrocities.

So never mind the bad weather, ladies and gentlemen, and mind your head Alice, we're stepping through the door, and the red buttons are very carefully arrayed, to trigger orbital bombardment:

(She's screaming)

(And I push the button)
(And later, she pushed the others)

52.

Some dark holes you don't get out of; that's why they exist; they're one-way gates, not to Hell, because Hell is merely this place underground. Underground is nice; it's how we survived the asteroid. Where all the roots are.

Who are you going to become once you climb in?

My name
My face
My awareness
My history
My family
All taken
Erased

In the great white saga of memory, now heaving its ship onto my horizon, over my eyes under the ground. Heal me Alice, for my manhood is gone, and my name and manners, my ways, oaks, rigidities, passages pearls and patiences, now gone, taken, and you are here, White Alice, underneath my eaves is your face, under the ground your bones, and I can hear you, gnawing and gnawing on them, to get the last gravy.

Here we are.

The Wasteland, not one in writing nor one in reality, but within: the inner waste, laid barren, after the electroshock.

Heal me, for I do not exist no longer, no more

me to use, and I am a

[ ]

what is it

this

[ ]

potent mark, or vestibule. This body. The body survives even though the mind does not. The mind is erased, and in erasure discovers its meaning: in palimpsest.

Each echo striving for new meaning.

Each scratch of skull on my face the architecture of a body foreign to archaeology, foreign to Man, the shape of the skull not human but divine, in the mind of a priest:

Bless me, Alice, for I have sinned, and I am foreign to confession, and underground where we invented wheat we invented prayer, and submission, and electroshock.

I know our masters are near; this is why I write this; to honor them; to know their cruelty; to advise them in the keeping of their specimens; to wait and word and hedge the ordure of being to know which casement will cry out to my name, like the death body in a future replicant's clone drinking its own blood in a medical basement, we are the Cauldron Born of History, the Mad Ants Underground, the White Race, the ugly mothers, and bad daddies, who invented civilization as we know it.

Civilization is hell.

Underneath the dark hole, patience becomes some other kind of man, like Solzhenitsyn watching the man with the cigarette watching the man who wants it, knowing never to look.

Look away, son, and all shall be given ye, but never look, at what we are.

Heal me, Alice, for this is Hell and you are my bounty, given to me even as sanity is, an inheritance, to spend as you will, to make much of or burn.

Burn the village and save its soul, Alice, and burn reality down around you and you will find me there, against and alone beneath this Earth, falling still faster, after you:

Oh now if I should bear it, bear it so deeply beneath you, underneath the waves and the sun, underneath the shadow of the valley of life, beneath my dreams and in yours, if I should bear it, Sisyphus to Ephyra again, riding a broken and ill-mannered nag of gold, camp followers all, the sun, moon, and stars, the black sky and your face, covered in tears:

53.

I remember now; who was it said that thing they said; but that wasn't what I wanted to say.

They're evil; and I will forget what they said.

What I remember is the ocean below me.

In some ways it was there I realized it was not about Alice, but about me. I had made myself come there; refuted authority and called upon my own; insisted and fought and been defeated and made into a prisoner and this, my punishment, was a beautiful thing, for it was a journey.

This has been the story of my exile and I can say with some certainty that exile is one of the best stories in the world.

But it exists only in the telling: when I cease to narrate, the last chapter of my resistance, the final minutes of my broadcast into the night, will go and leave me with this aftermath.

The ocean was below me and I was on their craft and they prodded me with another ultimatum: do our bidding, or "jump," be forced over the side.

If I can force powerful beings into ultimatums and get them to expend energy to eliminate me, torture me, hinder, poison and harry me, I can do other things, and this is the lesson of the exile: you have been rewarded, and this is your bequeathement: a new life.

54.

Now and an unleavening, whoever art made foul friendless and bonded to the gruesome work of our bondage, made new and holy, made savage, and fused to the infrastructure of the universe, warrior:

We are slipping away from the planet.

Alice, I am only a man, but I have become something else too: this thing that looked for you, the aspect and the shadow of it, curving through the ice storm, a ballistic arc of fire, this thing that is murder, and all of its variants, but then, that is only what men are. Perhaps what I mean to say is: here above the killing, I'm learning what it is to be a man.

The fires burning are like empires, receding in waves away from the Mediterranean, burning spires, cities and nations curling under the white hot mass of the drivers, spinning as they fall below us.

Make me your own and grip tight on the leash of your womanhood, the air and honor of it, mercurial focused and right, centered over the dove of your forehead, this meditation weighted and forlorn, hereout mastered but still this free thing, and so masterless:

Your will.

Be it your will; and we will go it, woman, because it is improbable and not nearly enough, nor will ever be.

I can count the dead, one for every billion:

One. Two. Three. Four. Five.

Lighting up underneath us.

Death is the most beautiful thing there is; but only because it is a reminder how small our universe.

Small like a woman's arms, and hopes, breeding the possibility of the sky.

Each raptured woman, scintil wavering over the fog and lakesky, is my own heart, now bleeding, because I am a mass murderer, and because I am in love.

55.

"What have you done!"

"We're leaving."

I take her down to the escape pods and tie her into the station and program the coordinates for our home planet.

I make the sign of the Black King over the air-lock as I seal it, black paint on steel, as a kind of curse, and also a historical marker, here he was again, here once again, here so many died and were ruined, under the shadowy sky of his per-turbation, driplet and drop into the steamy waters of his mind:

She's crying and I turn away to watch us spin out, and down, into the blue fire of our passage through the wormhole and through into the lim-itless dark.

56.

Shift and move, son, turn and weight, your body and my body in counterrhythm here hold the power of the universe, which is only a banyan waiting for the right moment, to breathe:

Breathe.

gasp

In each semaphore and sign I am there, no longer reachable—it is true I am gone, not to return—but still here, in my record of it.

This is the record of the record that was before it ended; who I was and thought to become but did not, and who I became, this will and arc out:

"Will you remember us in dreams?" the village people ask.

"Yes, of course."

I am a kind of robot resurrected after a certain number of aeons; perhaps only two, though it may have been as many as four. Like the Hindus we wait for it to cycle back around:

"Wait for it, son, wait for it . . ."

I have a son. Whatever that means. Anyway the word means boy, whatever my relation to him. Guidance counselor. Improbable guard. Jailer. Stalker and enemy. Father and son.

We are practicing the discipline of balance, one which is helpful to certain colonies subject to attack; each position of our arms determines the posture of the defense systems in this orbit.

Spinning around in the weightless shimmering dark.

"Breathe."

"Oh my god."

"You liked that one, huh?"

57.

My masters have relinquished control; which is another way of saying I have relinquished control. It is a mistake to imagine we are separate.

Who is took me here? Who took my hand, myself, and brought me here, to my city, and insisted I look, here about and through, to the chord tied to my hand, and to the world?

It may be that Alice does not even exist; or, if she does, she exists as much as I do, the holy ghost.

I am the holy ghost, set to haunt your city in my dreams, and yours.

This is my revelation: I am still here. I am not dead yet.

These words are mine; and though they are others too, I have made them. All that I thought I would find is gone; but I have found other things.

Who is it trembling in the night, trembling over me in my bedroom?

You, dark emperor, my body; take me, my dark emperor my body and lead me into the night, whose pitch and yaw will make me yours, ignited, burning for you over the strolls and causeways of Los Angeles, dead in midnight, and without fear.

Who is burning Los Angeles? Igniting it like a sun? Why did you bring me here, to hover round its edges, Mercury to her limbic smile?

58.

In the Korean barber's

We're waiting for word, of how it will be. Who is it took the laughter down, and made it the highway, suffering the weight of the cars and trucks and people, arguing over the shapes of the trees, the callow angle of the walk of the pedestrians, insisting on their right to forget, all we have done?

She moves her hands through my hair, and argues with her husband. Outside, the eclipse is approaching and some children wait with their viewing glasses, squinting into the bright air.

The old woman is reading her Redbook, staring over the years and the cities.

We're moving west, out of Los Angeles, over the sun and through it, over the night and down under the vessel of our secret Angeleno dawn, in death.

For though I have destroyed my city, burned it to ash, and all of its people, I have also escaped with it; taken it as my trophy in my secret kingdom, where it will never die.

"Short or medium?"

"Medium."

59.

Effie is singing, of all that it meant. Inside the café where the lights are falling dark and the light hovers over her face, a map of our destination, in Troy.

Hear her voice. As though it were the last thing you would ever hear.

In the Trojan night, far away, she is singing for us, seeking the causeway, of our connection.

Hacker trying the night halls, for the timely break, mark sent to the meeting ground to deliver a message we're all grateful for.

Effie—Kalfour's daughter—is singing.

There are no words to her song; or none that I will record here.

It was a song of regret; but also ambition, because that is our dual nature, myself and my companions, the losers who escaped.

Shimmering over us is the lighting effects wizardry of the proprietor, a loser like us, bent on taking us out from Los Angeles and history, away from Athens and our dark mooring of this continent, into the world we are only now coming to see.

In my world Iphigenia lived;

60.

In ancient times, and in some regions into the present, the lord was named after the place, so as to be seen as indistinguishable from it. Land and king.

In my world men are also named after places, in similar fashion, but not as rulers; rather we are benefactors of the idea of this kingdom.

So when I am Kalfour I see to its needs; and when I am Los Angeles I attack its (as no city loves to be denied like Los Angeles).

Perhaps there is no separation; I see I may be mistaken. Whether time does exist and we move through it, changing, or if instead that is illusion and we wear the same costume for eternity I cannot say. Both things may be true.

What I am trying to do is atone for my mistakes. And though this is a confession, it is also a battle plan for our revenge.

War is revenge; just or not. For all the time spent waiting.

- -

Obey, and all will be well. All manner of things will be well. You are in our trust.

I am ignited, and though I burn, I will light the way. We are descending.

These marks show other vessels; other trials and triangulators; the adjutants who marked their lives into the rock as we do now.

Descend and wait; just around the bend; just behind the door; just over the meniscus of time; just underneath your seat; just after the end of the sentence; just inside the book; underneath the black mark of my name; behind our city:

Descend and wait; music who hears us shall arbitrate the dignification of our event, anomalous but still noted, named and recorded in the fall of our life:

Descend and look, at all the armaments and years; my feet; my daughter.

Just over the lip of the horizon. Just behind my hand; under your waist; beneath your tongue the key; my lock; your voice; and all we became there; it is still with me; my arbitrary tribe

You my arbitrary tribe are lonely; holy; ignoble; ferocious; the long lamb of the long dark; my own; each hour of you fills me with sadness and regret; the mourning of this ambient awareness; stirring the dark borderland of our feet; and shuffling through; here now; recumbent; mending the vessels of feet in work; under the roof of the earth.

It's here; above and hereout; old Hades.

Perhaps he is still here and does not want to be seen.

(After all, his name means "invisible.")

What invisible dark things are ours are known to us, though not mentioned; and I insist on their right to be seen, not with eyes but ears, for our music is the best of us and I will use it as I use you—may I be forgiven—to find my daughter Iphigenia.

Effie knows I am coming and does not want to be found.

And when I locate her you will be rewarded.

61.

Here at the station plaza, they've chained all the chairs together around the tables, so that they look nice from a distance but you're unable to sit in them.

Only one in a long series of humiliations over centuries. The curtailing of public space. The curtailing of the public mind. Finally when we are unable to move we can be milked of our blood and then disposed of.

Of course this too is an illusion: they insist we grow stronger. They know these humiliations will destroy them and that is what they want, as Cronus did Uranus, and Zeus Cronus. But we are not yet strong enough to wield Saturn's sickle.

Was it that most Gnostics wanted to escape from the world? Is that why they posited that the universe is a lie? Or did they instead want to go deeper into this world, with all its illusions. Perhaps there is no difference.

Certainly, in my travels into the deep parts, I have felt I was leaving it all behind.

Yet here we remain. Of course my confession—this atonement—is also implicated in the masterful and cruel illusion. What do I expect from you? Understanding—but what then?

Perhaps understanding is enough. Understanding that surpasseth understanding. Ha ha ha.

Alice does not like Los Angeles. She sits here by me, staring at the fountain. Like a ghost, though she is real. Perhaps we are both ghosts. We sit on a bench, since the chairs have been locked down. We drink our coffee. Still these privileges are permitted to us.

I am fortunate to be a citizen of a country whose carcass is slowly being picked clean. We shall arise as bones, free from the burdens of our flesh, bent with a singular will on that greater atonement, children rising off the altar and taking hold of Abraham's hand, and removing it from his body.

When he is dead the Earth will flourish once again.

I will die but I suspect I will die before I do, in a passion that exceeds my understanding, traversing me like a wave and leaving me broken, undone, and punished into humility; transformed.

- -

There is no escape from it. Why should I care so much about escape?

What would it me for me to escape?

Perhaps it would mean that I became someone else. A different body, or even this body slightly modified. Aged. Perhaps aging is one form of escape.

- -

I am behooved (if I can say that) here in the

dungeon, which is actually on the 6th floor, under the square fluorescents, over the sea of our lies, indignant but still potent, looming delicately over us like a beautiful ruin: administration.

We fit well into our slots, like harried well-weathered components, waiting to be activated in the computer of university.

The Department of Human Security expresses through its agent its enduring love and devotion, which necessitates our obedience.

Well, they get it anyway. We seem to relish it. It is after all what we were manufactured for. Outside the moon is moving over the sun, endeavoring to reveal the dreamworld we inhabit.

It asks that we awake, under its murderous curtain, and see.

- -

The train and the train run at night and the train runs at night on the train whose train lifts us over the edge charges us filling moving circumventing and observing the various exits, none of them accessible.

The train moves us south over itself, marks the markings of itself, and marks us. The train knows why. We are not certain; are burdened in incomplete knowledge, luxuriously acquainted with these many absences.

The train running at night observes us, marks us and knows, subsists in the knowledge we'll come to know it, marking its tracks, serpent-like, over the sky.

The huge machine of our awareness still huddles under the mighty train, who moves out and over it, beyond it.

I may go into it, and be delivered, though the thought terrifies me.

I could be delivered from all this. Delivered over the edge and through into the canyon of sky whose breath tempts me, maddening me, nearby but not for me.

I can't go on this train. Not without Alice.

- -

We've engaged in a project beyond our imagining, almost by definition. We can flirt with the edges; cast out lines. Peer over the edge.

Have dreams. Work to forget the intimation of the boundary areas, the portals out and to points beyond that bear their fruit in our hearts, but:

Being here, awake here, poses its own set of difficulties even if we do forget, have forgotten; never knew.

62.

Now worlds apart I will not leave; cannot; will not; arbor or arbitrary; at light.

This darkness will not heal me but it will not let me die; she is speaking in the dark, over the light.

Prescience or fecundity and the bright water strums my feelings underground, shaking my body to speak.

These and these and these here, bright barnacles over my raft:

We're leaving.

Now I will confess everything. And though I lie it is one of the truer lies I will tell; something the aliens themselves do not know.

I will not leave I'm leaving; my mast.

I will not leave; I'm leaving; my heart.

"What is it you think you will accomplish, Robin?"

Not a what but a where.

I will accomplish a where.

Where each island holds me down, pulling me under, through and under the water, back and into the water, whose voice will remember me, even in death, unstoppable and monarchic, queen of the waters of the river, barrow-fed and rich with feed, arch and weight and ballast, broke over my hands, for you, my love;

63.

Of course, all in all this is quite ordinary. Even though it is my job to recreate the strangeness in ordinary things sometimes the power escapes me, and then they seem dross, the useless life-matter I am surrounded with, through no choice of my own, and having very little choice about when or how to leave it.

My routine, insofar as it resembles many others, also acts as vaccination against beginning (and completing) this work, as I remain tied to this idea that writing is supposed to be original.

Aboriginal, even. And mine is neither.

Inside the routinized mind of Man, who is it going about his head, to strut and fret not for an hour but for years, performing religious obeisance to the shower, toilet, subway, Starbucks, and wage labor?

What kind of man is it—and what kind of woman—inebriated in the routine, hum and drum humdrum, this humming drum, weaponized in its lethal subservience to reality, ordinating cause, effect and show, liberating the mind from matter and setting us on our feet, puppets for the dance?

The ordinary man. The ordinated man. Ordinal man. Coordinated man. Ordinateur.

For if I should complete the sum of our embrace, whose sigil should arise to commute our sentences, as numbers for Pythagoras dancing as gods, leashing us onto our great train—

Alice is gone. Only the crow is here, to remind me that she ever existed. Sad, funny, crow, smiling at me from the tree, suspecting our dark audience is coming to a close:

- -

We're in the ark again, whose method is arcane, shut under the doorstep of our world, to weather out its feelings of difference. In the maelstrom of reality we are the judges, deciding life from death, hope from despair, and the weight of the earth from our double-weight, ourselves, locked in the lobby to decide the father, and all fathers.

That moment of decision, like the moment of writing, is holy.

- -

We're undertaking a journey but I don't know where we're going. My students and I. They have me teaching again—improbably, perhaps, but the assignment seems sincere.

We sit down and write together in silence, the only sounds a woman's heels in the hallway.

- -

We won't escape—not now. I could give any reason but it wouldn't be enough. Perhaps there are no reasons.

Nor can we make peace with such a fate—our goal is to be driven mad, and seduced into ever greater heights of hypocrisy—believe new absurdities, commit new atrocities, shark to school and back again and reverse, subject to unspeakable predations and ritual torture, circling faster and faster around The Eye, which becomes more and more difficult to see...

64.

We can take it any way you want. Sit down and shoot it out; love each other to death. It's a beautiful night, with the stars in their place, over your head, and under your eyes.

We can take it anywhere you want; over the moon, a pizza pie, over your heart.

It's all right; I know how it is. How you made it feel. How you've been, hovering over the abyss. How long it's been. Hovering, hovering, through the madness, in all colors.

We can bake it any way you want; over the cap; over the nose; on the wall; in time for tea; the max weight and the best surprise, with frosting and toes, with your nose on my ear; this leer for you too:

We can make it any way you want; over your bottom; over your top; this flop is still uptight right; we can make it; shake it and fake it until it looks just like the others; feels just like the others.

We can divine the song; who is yours; who makes yours; who shouts yours; over the cage of your life; over the striving of your life; over your bondage the bright stream of the truth will ignite the sky; I can see it; breathing; next to you, my love.

It won't be long. This aegis of longing. Aegis of trust who must confess the truth, must obsess the truth, the ruth and pearl of our gleanings from the flock of the dark beneath our feet, this meetly meat, morose and thick slick with fluids undercome with broad beats and backs and marriages no marriages no more;

It won't be punishing or hateful, not pitiful or graceful but this clumsy fuck underneath the store, over the gourd and beneath the bench, the wrench of the fjord, humming daily, cumming daily, for the march;

March and march;

March on;

This is your daily gravy; mountain sustenance and rocks and moss; the cock and the walk and the stars betake themselves railing and ranting over your shoulder; for us:

Who made it so and who made it care; who made it this color; red and white; blue and black; lacking the number of the cairn the burial rite of the bear; who made the air; in your tongue?

Was it you?

Who made the brack and bright who made the raft and tight cantilevered dum and dun drug and bun your hearse and midnight screech my love the arbor heard all over the marsh;

Who made it come and keep the awl and ear and earl for our wordings worlding the vowel gap and pearl my love; who made the eel and ruckage roughage reaping the moon the mule and our flock who made the agent and the emblem the meaning and the pageant pitiful but savage shirking and delivering the music underdone but still risen, cambling caustic and mad, my dearest love;

Who made it shiver in the night; when you were bright as the stones; who made this thrum, locked and agitated, boring and batches and batches; striving for the hamper, for the chalk, for the mark and the balk, to sail free into the eye, into the hand.

Into my hand; who made the handle; inside your fleece; the neighbor dancer of my eardred my dear eardred ornery eardred locking the luminous spire of dreams and dooms whoever may keep them I give it you, my love, this umber guard, to make you wait; to make you strum

Strum my gum for me; strum my love for me; who hated it; strum my lumber and brum for me; so near;

and gleaning—

Who made this asp and your barber; your bedded bender bolter box and kosher map and rover dell the reef of your long coal, smoldering hot, keeping close to the movements of the aisle, around me, this wood and this pearl, of night:

Who rasps the midnight oil with the kaleidoscope colliding so near our bed; shattering the salient night; who made you deliver rum and gin; brooms and bins; books and then more books; thousands of books; streaming over your eyes;

who made you cheer, to the aliens near, to the
dear hearts and hatreds close to the gout and mull
of our month;
Was it still you?
Who made the demons come; vast and insis-
tent; who made us dive?
All into the water.
I can still see you
panting
making the song in your walk
it's still you
isn't it
still you
over the pavement
over the silent pavement
shaking the music out of your eyes
out of your nose
this religious music from your gums and fin-
gertips
startling and solid and new
the placid cuff of the mewling herd circling
about the watery rock in the heath, licking the
foliage of your beard; trying to hold on; over the
nearness of it—this beating nearness—
I saw how far you had fallen and how dear it
would be for me to carry you back up:

65.

Man, in needing woman, surrenders to that inadequacy in himself, not only the biology but the arrow of it, like a black wave of light, at right angles to the way we see the world, convulsing over the bright white street. Ying and yang, yes yes, but also:

The worldlessness of belonging; exterior to reality, and its circumpolar visits, arbitrations and divine signals, exterior to the presence of the self, not only its body and mind but also this gravity, humming around the envelope of the spirit, intoxifying the periodicity of one's emotions, cycling faster around her

All perfectly quotidian. Why remark on it at all. Why make these marks whose name will not be told to me, no matter how many gods I slay in the daylight, planets I bomb, governments I overthrow or worlds I inhabit or reinhabit; no matter who I become I cannot remember my name.

In this Robin is merely my amanuensis. My needs as Kalfour, that title, approach this thing, but they too are inadequate.

Man in needing woman approaches the shell of the sphere of the world, the system of the world, herded into the maze, over the quadrant and set spinning, ye child's top, dradle dradle dradle I made it out of clay and when it's wet and ready:

Unburdening the limelight of the soul we drift

over the aegis of black waves, my spirit more sodden than my cloak; my eyes still seeing that other world we have left behind.

No rabbit hole no more.

Man in needing woman find that his name too is meaningless; no descriptor in the world can reduce it, nor hedge it against need, nor deliver it when needed, nor manage to excuse or calcify it, run it over or under (but through—yes, we can be run through).

Not needing any description we're left with our duties, laziness not withstanding its shape the crowded vessel of our years. Hurriedly jettisoning; bailing, pumping bilge, watching for fish.

Each fish fills with me a religion; it is a sprite like no other. Sometimes I catch and eat them and Alice is happy then for a while; until she is hungry again.

Just feeding the woman over and over; this is clearly our job. Even a machine could do it, and that's what we are. Some huge machine, unreckonable in size, not too dainty or in need of maintenance, merely obstreperous in our hesitation to deliver the available pieces of the puzzle because—well, who knows what might be next? Can't we hold something back?

Does she want us to hold something back?

The Black King of Kalfour arises. Brushes his hair. Delivers the affidavit to the counselor. Rises on his step to summon the messenger spirit and hands it to the creature, who smiles in its evil fashion; not drinking too bright; not bowing too low; not nearing too much the season of it; not howling until visible; not naming the world; undressing; leering into the moonlight the Black King, unfolded; his patter the alma mater of several years, climbing the wool of my back, shouting out my window into the street—

"You there! What time is it!"

"What?"

"I say, what time is it!"

"It's . . . it's about twelve o'clock . . ."

"Twelve! Twelve mighty lessons! My god . . ."

I can't hush the beast; he's holding on to my hair. Who went to who—in the articulation of possession, as in marriage, which first or second may have some narrative quality but no experiential one of any kind: we cannot know who is in charge, amanuensis or author, god or mortal, emblem or thing itself, noxious and true and pouring over my body;

Alice is laughing and I cannot remember how it is I ever met her; nor what it is I mean to do with her once I –

Once I take her to bed—

Once I love her—

Once this time and once that time—who was it—it was me—but that one, that one, that one needed words, and reasons, and do I still need them?

"Are you all right, honey?" she asks. And I'll say, "of course" or "yes." And smile.

But I have no reason to grasp even on to the shape of it; what could it mean; who would it entail; and what time have I landed in now?

Are we returning to my kingdom or leaving it? Am I rescuing her or bringing her to my prison?

And my masters.

What is it my masters want. Are they still here? Have I been abandoned?

Am I free?

My name, won't you tell me—
my name, what is it?
Tell me what it is—

66.

We're shaking terribly under the mast; shaking and shaking.

67.

Administration is its own right—the art of appearances. Certainly Augustus must have known this better than anyone, who paid cash on the nail for his grand works, to the greater glory of Rome.

In its minutiae—door hinges, building ledges, lines of sight and areas of reflection (here I am looking at the Water Administration Building of Los Angeles), we can perceive its central agitation, fear, reserve and hope: that all things shall be well, all manner of things...

Yet what can wellness mean here, in administration? Less glamorous than leadership, administration is the logistics of society-as-war, the arms and hands, no matter the uniform—a minister is a hand.

The art of administration lies in being both perfectly ordinary—perfectly visible—and completely secretive. The prestidigitation of rulership, where the building is not a building but almost literally a house of cards, no matter the permanence of the stone, it is rearranged before the eye can discern the tower's collapse ... its golden sun raiment not illusion but a simple distraction (away from the brutality of empire) but also a road towards the etherealness of it all—almost not really here—an evocation, almost a kind of illness.

That the building itself should have drawn me here now seems almost inevitable—it cannot have been Hollywood, not really, not some story heard at night on the dark screen but this ineffable monument, the great beauty of Kafka, Los Angeles, whose pure white burka shines over the world: huge, fecund, ripe with history and blood, unknowable, its order equivalent not to the ether dreams of the movies but the things themselves: your thoughts.

Thoughts raised up, over, beyond, and through you, rattling you in a cage as you are awarded a view like nothing you have ever seen: the right arm of the king.

The beauty of administration is that it is invisible, even though she stands there, an eager servant with her broom, performing the dignified and necessary work of sweeping the square clean, her inner squares simultaneously extend outward, boxing you in: as David Icke would have it, the cube of Saturn is everywhere, Kaaba, Hellraiser and El Sereno, shut into the tumultuous light of god, nearing my lips, on our bough-tip over the sea's waters, on our concrete river, I and my love, dead to the world, regard our new mission:

Warden.

Wardeness of All of Wonderland.

- -

What we are beginning, I cannot say, though I can be sure now that we are beginning. There's that anticipation—tingling in the head, tightening the gut—suggesting that the big cat is going to come over the rise, with its bright green eyes.

In a way I am almost ashamed of the excitement—perhaps this is how London felt during the Blitz, terrified and thrilled at once.

Each new moment does fill me with terror—of who I am becoming.

Alice seems to be unchanged.

I realize now the center of this confession: it was never about Alice. It was about me. Whether I loved her or not is irrelevant—I know that she never really loved me.

68.

I who am Kalfour begin to dance; I am dancing.

Kalfour dances, ranging out into the night for instruments; over my many quarries; into the beds and lorries of the unfallen, to invite them in:

Kalfour ranges over the enemies of my heart, like children stepping over the world, rock, mica and range of earth, the will of the wild of the day, shuttered behind our will:

I unlock the wood and screw and open us onto the divide between rich and poor; onto the scrape of the stone who makes me my battle kingdom; each in his own element; and mine in prison.

This is my prison; I am Kalfour; the so-called Black King; and if it is my wish I will have you my horse to ride, here at the crossroads of the ordinary and the divine, we have dancing, messieurs and mesdames, who art with you, in your blood, open your veins!

This is my kingdom of blood. My holy raiment, of blood.

And if you wash me in blood I am healed; revenged; made known and new; made aspirant; made this wish in foil and over the target season of my aspirations; made leering and unknowable; made yours; I am Kalfour; Black; noble and untrue, and in my revenges I seek knowledge and understanding, of how to kill you.

There will be so many ways.

I am dancing in my heart; here in my prison kingdom: to set the meter to our shared crown, our holy miter, of liberation:

One foot in front of the other.

One child in front of the other.

One meaning in front of an another.

In place of the child, a manuscript.

In place of the manuscript, the hidden world.

Here my hidden world, envelope, should burn, but I carry its ashes to you, my love, who burned with me. Though we are gone I have become, in the aphorism, more powerful than you could possibly imagine, which is only to say: a sun, screaming impotent over the soundless valleys of my unassailable position in the skies of this world, now bent to serve its will, and watch its fate, warm its valleys and rivers and usher in the cast of my thought; here now my love though you have gone I will seek to carry the muster of your feeling into the celebration of this day; new again; new once again; in my bayonet and Baikonur moustache; bowsprit and bocage; my boutonnière:

We can't hold in the thresh.

Thresh me, thrush, knocking the world, and I will have done with it, whenever you say, whenever you say we are done and I will close up the night and sink my castle under the sea to dream things which I will never be able to tell.

Tell me we are there. That I will do it. That I needn't think of you again.

Whose holy, where it was, in my dreams, should have been there, my tooth, or scroll, this dance itself; for Robin.

We can pity him in the normalcy of his rounds; still creeping over the edge when we have long fallen over it and through. Still weeping for the cause of it all, and its beauty.

Yes it should have been holy earlier, for I was wrong; wrong to have insisted so hard on the beating of my one drum, for there are many; so many I have discovered; countless, and I cannot recount even a fraction of them, but even if it is true, where that holy sprite and spirit was that I encountered and imprisoned into myself in my investiture and coronation, still I can see how far it might still carry; that even if I was wrong I was in the right place, with words that may have been close to right; close enough to evoke some shadow of the thing I had dreamt of, in my body, waiting here for the moment:

[Well, we've arrived. Things are not anything like I had hoped.

Obviously the rabbit hole extends into Los Angeles.

Alice has gotten a job as a waitress on Sunset Boulevard and I have been assigned a class at university, teaching the Epic of Gilgamesh.

The students are remarkably strong-willed—admirably so. I wish I had been as tough at their age. I know I was very soft.]

I who am Kalfour begin to dance, so as to describe the reasons for my earlier refusals, dancing around it, moving closer to it, asymptotic to the origin of the divine, my heart, wintered and caustic, dwelling over the peer water, watching for snakes.

Refuse power and get under the dwelling, leave it behind, forget, betray and set under the swelling mast of your past, too horrible to contemplate—this was my plan—slow drip unwilling to drop . . .

I am dropping; this is my power; in the fall through the hole and down and through:

Los Angeles has so many enemies; many of them its residents, and I amongst them. Its rabbits number in the thousands, vibrating their turn signals under the eye of God, and though they are late, they do not rush, because it is always glorious to be late to a meeting, to suggest the heliopause between your subsumation of reality and all other suns, circling around galactic center wondering—in wind-up—is this my chance?

Will I be fulfilled?

Will I be fulfilled, Kalfour, Fourth in the Line,

triumphant, my heart, will I be reprieved, triumphant, over my troubled star, will I make music as I ought, each avenue reprised and fought over like a lion; magic, maelstrom; my main demand and mouse; disguising my shuttering away:

(fleeing on little white feet)

Will I be delivered. Known.

In this I am already beyond my city; its heliopause already disappointing before my more quasar-like shudderings, shirking the glad hand of its darkness for some deeper communion, in my Alice:

Like all the women of Los Angeles Alice is dark, meditating over the void between her desires and what is possible, and what she is willing to betray.

Like all the women of Los Angeles Alice is huge, strumming her gravity as epochal firespheres stuck in the light on the sidewalk, bending light;

Like all the women here she's waiting.

Waiting;

Waiting;

Not for me. Nor any man. I do not know what they are waiting for.

69.

Bacon and cheese on medium rare. Hold the mayo.

Kale chips and an IPA; stir fry tofu and aioli toast; couscous over garlic rye; the leering light of the Boulevard its own daemonic awareness greater than any Hollywood producer, who haven't been coming in lately anyway—

Ash Wednesday; Eid Mubarak; Labor Day and American Film Market, coasting on the afterglow of the revolution, perhaps even the Roman Empire, in its Italian eye; staring at the women, and wondering;

wondering;
where does it stop
who am I now
is it this minute
this hour
that I am appointed tribune
that my tribunal
will be seated in the rotunda
over the swath of bodies
within the circle of women
my veggie burger is ready
my toga is tinged with violet
Ramnes,
Tities,
Luceres,
founding tribes of Rome,

with Etruscan eyes and Greek hands
Egyptian feet
The shadow of a Jewish god
(sans meteorite)
hovering over coffee
making a window onto the salad
dignifying an off-color joke
with an awareness of the historical context
the business angle of the annual feast
courted to become beautiful
like my curried avocado garnish

I am so close to the sun I am like him;
Unable to stand the world;
Unable even to see it;
Showering the street with light

70.

Alice is serving lunch; one step and two, over the floor, drinking in the moments of theater, not-actress actress, performing work.

In the eddy of this river comes Los Angeles, lurking quiet in the shade, dark and majestic water, eddying; eddying;

Break and match the heat, the weight, the step and scour in the cool pale night;

who heard the bright light, baleful and unheard till now, who carries the mare, shirked shadowed and uncomely, her heart, to the cool pale water of the night under our concrete barren hillside, shadowing the grace of our hundred deaths;

A fair number in Los Angeles. You could have more. It's only an eddy, you know.

Watching the clock. Watching her heart.

Our bereavement should not be surprising to us and yet it is; at least to me.

That escape should leave so much of you behind.

Like those ancient Greek exiles, unable ever to speak of anything again but their home.

Yet in my case at least it was never my home; never anywhere; never but the signal over my noise; dropping paper; coursing and caressing the mass of me.

Who makes this night for us, shaken and regarded as mad, mad pale storm; fires burning in the scorched hills, killing us; waiting for us to mourn it, praise it, worship it, no fire department no more.

It is all right; it is appropriate; here in the Eddy.

Circling slow around the calm clear center of the bank.

She calls me from the last payphone on the west side to say I will never see her again.

71.

What wilderness is mine is something I embrace; whoever should fold it; caress it; make it known in the kingdom of Kalfour; who is my heart.

About the author

Robin Wyatt Dunn was born in Wyoming in 1979. He is a graduate student in creative writing at the University of New Brunswick, Canada.

www.ingramcontent.com/pod-product-compliance
Lightning Source LLC
Chambersburg PA
CBHW051511260626
47162CB00008B/2923